THE CHRISTMAS ORPHAN

ROSIE DARLING

PROLOGUE

"Why did you give that lady your coins, Father?" Jane Walker asked. "Was it her Christmas present?"

James Walker smiled down at his innocent daughter. She was just five and understood little about the world.

He was glad because James knew that the world, and London in particular, could be a terrible place. He would protect her from it for as long as he could.

"No, my darling little girl. That lady was very poor. She had no money for food. We have enough money, so I gave her some of ours," James replied slowly. "I would have given the coins to her no matter what the day."

Jane thought about his answer for a moment. "Why does she have no money for food? Is she a bad lady? Is that why she was dirty?"

James wondered how he could explain how some people had nothing in this world and that there was little chance or hope for them. He decided that he could not. When he didn't understand how horrific life could be for the downtrodden, how could he possibly hope to explain it to his beautiful young daughter?

"She was dirty because she has no place to live. She does not live in a nice house as we do. We wake up each morning and wash with warm water and soap. That poor lady is not able to do that. So, we try to help where we can. We understand that one day we might be poor, and we would want people to help us. Does that make sense?"

Jane considered for a moment, "Yes, Father. Is that why Mama went to help those people after church?"

"It is. She will be home soon, and we can enjoy Christmas Day together. And after dinner, you will get your Christmas present."

Jane's eyes shone at that prospect. She had been a little upset to learn that her mother would leave them for a few hours on Christmas Day. She wanted everyone to be together.

"I'm cold, Father," she shivered after they had walked in silence for almost a minute.

James agreed that it was perishingly cold. It was the coldest winter that even he could remember. Reports from further up the river were that the Thames had frozen. There was talk of having a frost fair as they used to in the old days. Market stalls would be erected on the frozen river. People would ice-skate. There would be plays, games and hog roasts. James had never seen a frost fair, but his grandmother used to talk about them often over the long winters. He was sure they would be an incredible sight. Half of him wished it would get colder still so the river might freeze deeper further downstream. But the other half of him knew that if it did, so many more people would suffer.

They had attended church at St Mary's that Christmas morning. James's wife, Rose, had gone to help the churchgoers serve hot soup and bread to the very poorest of the community. It was something she did every year.

James and Jane had gone to watch the carollers in the square. They had eaten roasted chestnuts hot off the fire and were now slowly walking home through the park. Holly was the only sign of life amidst the snow and ice.

"We'll be home soon enough," James said. "Come on, shall we cut some holly to decorate our front door?"

"Can we, Father?" exclaimed an excited Jane, jumping up and down.

"Of course." James walked over to the nearest bush and pulled his switch knife from his pocket. He showed Jane how to carefully cut the sprig at a slight angle so that it would regrow. Jane loved flowers. Their house had a beautiful garden and Jane would spend hours in it during the summer as Rose carefully tended the flowers. Rose would cut flowers from the garden and Jane would pretend to sell them from a shop. He could often come home from work and give his daughter a few small coins in exchange for a rose that he would give to his own Rose. Jane said that one day she wanted a real flower shop in London. James hoped that his daughter's dream would one day become a reality.

As James gently pulled the holly cutting, he shook its covering of snow over Jane's head.

She laughed in delight.

"What is going on here then?" a female voice

spoke out.

James and Jane turned towards it.

"Mama," Jane shouted with delight and ran towards her.

Rose Walker engulfed her in a big hug and stroked her daughter's bright red cheeks. "You're freezing, little one."

"I am. But Father says we are going home now to have our Christmas dinner and open presents."

Rose laughed. "Your father is right. Have you got what you need, husband?"

"I have everything I need right here," James said lovingly.

The three walked together, Jane holding her parents' hands as they did so. Occasionally she would leap and her mother and father would playfully swing her and drop her into the snow. James carefully held his sprig of Holly in his other gloved hand.

In less than five minutes they were home.

James was a senior clerk at a merchant bank in the city. The Walkers were not rich, but they were comfortable. The house next to the park came with the job. James and Rose had discussed on more than one occasion the possibility of employing a cook or a maid. But they had always decided against it. They did not want someone else in their home, intruding upon their idyllic family life.

Instead, Rose handled most domestic matters personally. She would cook the family meals, go to the butcher and the market and address the day-to-day cleaning. She paid a lady to handle the laundry and once a week two young women would come in to do a deep clean of the house. It was the perfect arrangement.

James opened the door and Jane ran inside. The fires had been left to die down to embers, but there was still warmth. And there was the most wonderous aroma from the kitchen. Rose paused to help her husband weave the sprig of Holly around the bright brass knocker.

They stood back to admire it. "Merry Christmas," whispered James into his wife's ear and then he tenderly kissed her.

"Come on. No kissing" interrupted an almost indignant Jane. "I'm hungry."

They laughed and did as their child had bid them.

A little more than an hour later they were seated around the dining table. Jane could not believe the amount of food spread before them.

There was a roast goose and roast beef. There was cabbage, parsnips and carrots. Finally, there was the biggest pile of crisp roasted potatoes Jane had ever seen.

By the time they had eaten their fill, hardly a dent appeared to have been made on the food. They would be eating the leftovers for days.

"Presents, I think," said James with a smile, walking over to the Christmas tree in the corner of the room.

It was their first year having a Christmas tree. The Queen had a tree every year at the Palace. It was a tradition that the Prince Consort had brought with him from Germany. Ever since there had been an engraving of the royal family published standing around their own huge tree, the demand for Christmas trees had increased with every year. After pestering from Jane, James had finally agreed on one this Christmas.

James reached under and pulled out two boxes. A tall box for Jane and a smaller one for her mother. Rose walked over to the tree and pulled her own box out from under it.

"You first, Father," Jane said clapping her hands in excitement.

James carefully removed the brown paper from

around the box. It would be reused in some way. Unwrapping revealed a set of seven beautiful handkerchiefs, each embroidered in silver thread with his initials.

"This is a wonderful gift, thank you, both," James said stroking the raised W with his finger.

"Jane chose them," Rose said stroking her daughter's blonde hair softly.

"You are very clever, Jane," James said, smiling warmly.

Jane's eyes shone from the praise from her parents. "You next, Mama."

Rose smiled and carefully unwrapped the package from James. It was a jewellery box. Rose couldn't help but gasp when she opened it. It was a gold locket in the shape of a heart. Jane could see that it was engraved with the initials J and R intertwined.

She reached out and stroked James' large hand and there were tears in her eyes, "It's beautiful. Thank you."

Jane's excitement was now almost bubbling over.

"I think it must be your turn now, my precious angel," Rose said turning to her daughter.

Very slowly Jane undid the red bow that Rose

had tied around the parcel. She ran her fingers under the brown paper taking care not to rip it. She unfolded it and her eyes opened wide with wonder.

A perfect doll, almost a copy of Jane, stared back at her from a beautiful wooden box.

It was a doll she had been staring at in the window of an expensive shop that summer when she was out with her father. He had remembered and gone back to buy it for her.

"Thank you so much. Thank you, thank you, thank you." Jane rushed and smothered both her parents with kisses. "I shall call her Emily."

The rest of Christmas Day was perfect for the Walker family. James added more coal to the fire in front of which Jane played with Emily, enjoying the heat and the ambience. The flames danced on the new locket that now hung proudly around Rose's neck. Rose and James sipped on wine while they watched their daughter play. She was so engrossed that she had to be made to sit at the table and eat her figgy pudding.

When Rose was tucking into bed that night, she kissed her mother on the cheek and in a tired voice whispered, "I think Christmas might be the most perfect day ever."

CHAPTER 1

2 Years Later

Rose Walker bent to kiss her daughter's pale cheek. "Be careful now. Be back before dark."

Jane nodded, "Yes, Mama." She clutched the bundles of flowers to her chest. A cold wind whipped around her ears as she stepped out into Whitechapel Street.

Rose pulled the hood of Jane's cloak up over her red hair, "Good girl." She rubbed her swollen belly and shivered as a fierce gust of wind tunnelled through the alleyways. A fine rain began to fall, dampening the discoloured snow drifts that lined the road.

Jane gave her mother one last smile and turned to make her way through the crowded slum. She kept her eyes downcast as she walked, concentrating on avoiding potholes and enormous iced-up puddles. Walking with her eyes cast down also meant she could avoid seeing what was around her: the families on street corners with ragged, wailing children; the men with faces pocked with smallpox scars. Worst of all were the bodies of dead dogs and cats, their eyes glassy and lifeless. Once, Jane even saw the corpse of a man.

From that day on, she knew to always walk through Whitechapel with her eyes downcast, not looking up until the brass buckled boots of the passers-by told her she was out of the slums and within the section of the city where men did not curl up and die on the street.

Life had not always been this way. Jane had fond memories of the house in Islington next to the park. Memories of planting flowers in the garden with her mother. Memories of her father. Her first seven years of life had been carefree. She and her family had wanted for nothing.

But then her father died suddenly eight months

ago. The beautiful house with the garden had come with the job. Two months after James' death the bank had forced Rose and her daughter out. They had no heart.

James had saved a little money, but it was a small sum. The house and its contents had formed a considerable part of his compensation. A small death-in-service payment from the bank would see Rose and Jane though a few months. But Rose had another concern, and she was reluctant to spend what limited funds she had.

Rose found work in the grim factories in the hope of keeping her limited savings in the bank. Three months after her husband's death, she was sick first thing in the morning and she was forced to admit what she had suspected for over a month. She was carrying her dead husband's child. She knew she would not be able to keep her job for long.

Rose had found an almost reasonable room in a creaking Whitechapel tenement. She would keep the money for as long as she could. Their new home consisted of nothing but a single room with a crooked table and two chairs. James and Rose had been gifted a bed when they were wed which now stood in one corner and on which mother and daughter slept together.

IT PROVED to be a difficult pregnancy. Rose had lost her job at the factory after little more than a month.

WITH A LITTLE MONEY from their precious savings, they bought flowers for Jane to sell in the wealthier sectors of the city.

THERE WAS much that Jane hated about her new life, but she adored selling the flowers. She would feel a burst of joy when she clutched the precious bundles to her chest each morning. She loved the way the vibrant colours cut through the grey and gloom of the city around her. She loved the scents, the textures of the stems, and the fragile petals.

. . .

She had spent her first month of flower selling moving around the city, searching for the best place in which to sell them. She had found the perfect location; a square off Charlotte Street where the people lived in big white houses and walked by with pockets jangling with coin.

She taught herself the names of all the flowers she sold.

Lily

Bluebell

Rose, like her mother.

"Aren't you a clever girl?" her favourite customer, Mrs Cron, would say each time she bought flowers from Jane. Mrs Cron kept house for a wealthy family around the corner from the square. "One day I'm going to steal you and you'll come work for me."

Throughout the summer, Jane had come home with her own pockets jangling with coin. Her mother would greet her at the door and smile broadly as Jane handed over the money.

"You're a good girl, Jane," she would say, pressing a hand to her ever-growing belly. "Your little brother will be grateful his sister is such a talented flower seller."

"What if it's a girl?" Jane would ask each time.

"Then she will be very grateful too."

But as the days had grown shorter, Jane started to return home with her pockets emptier and emptier. The cold weather meant there were fewer flowers to sell. People began to decorate their houses with candles instead of colourful blooms. Today, Jane's arms were filled only with mistletoe and holly. It was all she had been selling for weeks now. But it was Christmas in two days and she was sure she could sell a few bunches of holly to decorate the festive dinner tables.

For the last two months winter had hit London hard. Snow had covered the ground for the best part of six weeks. With little money to spend on coal, Jane thought she would never be warm again. The bed had been sold a month before and now they slept on the mattress on the floor in front of the dying fire.

She stood in her usual place on the edge of the square and watched the carriages rattle down the street. She could see the people inside as they passed; women huddled in cloaks and muffs, men in top hats, their collars pulled to their chins.

Jane looked up to see the rain turning to snow. The tiny white flecks hung on her cloak and made her red hair glitter. She shivered, walking in a circle to try and keep warm.

Two men crossed the square, their heads bowed in conversation.

"Fresh flowers," Jane called, but they didn't look up. Her little voice disappeared into the thickening mist.

By midday, she had sold nothing but a few sprigs of holly. The snow was getting heavier, blanketing the city in a fresh cover of white. Despite its beauty, Jane didn't like the snow. It made the streets she knew feel unfamiliar and otherworldly and she worried that she would never find her way home.

As the pale sun began to dip towards the horizon, she began the long walk home, her little feet leaving prints in the fresh snow that covered the square.

Her arms were still full of flowers, her pockets empty of coin. She felt tears behind her eyes. She had wanted to come home with money for her mother and for the child Jane knew would arrive any day now. Though her mother had never said a thing, Jane knew they were running out of money. The stew they always ate for supper had become a watery broth. The night before, her mother had gone without dinner. She had claimed not to be hungry, but Jane knew the broth pot had been empty. She blinked away her tears. She would not cry. Not today. It was almost Christmas. Her favourite time of year. This year, of course, would be very different. They would not have her father. There would not be a Christmas tree with beautiful gifts under it. But they could still have a happy Christmas, couldn't they?

She hurried up the gloomy staircase of their tenement building. The wind whistled through the gaps in the wall, making her shiver. She pushed the door open to find their tenement room bare. The bed was gone, and their dishes and cups were gone. Her mother was bent over a battered duffel bag, folding their few clothes and setting them carefully inside.

She put down her armful of drooping flowers. "Mama? What are you doing?"

Rose looked up, a strained smile on her face. "Jane, my darling. How was your day?"

Jane pushed past her question. "Are we leaving?" she asked again, wrapping a coil of red hair around her finger.

"You're not to worry yourself, Jane. Everything will be all right."

"Are we going somewhere?"

Rose pressed a hand to her belly, "Just for a little while, my darling."

"But it's Christmas in two days, Mama."

Rose smiled again. Jane could see tears in her mother's eyes. Her mother had cried a lot since her father's death. It had been a long time, Jane realised since her mother had not been sad.

Rose picked up Emily, Jane's doll, and gently put it in the duffle bag.

She buckled the duffel bag closed and looked down at something in her fist. She gave Jane another strained smile. "Come here, my darling."

Rose knelt awkwardly and gripped Jane's hand. She pressed the object into her daughter's palm. Jane looked down. In her hand was her Mama's heart-shaped locket on the end of a gold chain. The initials J and R were still engraved on it, intertwined as if they have never been apart. She ran a finger over its smooth surface, allowing her nails to fall into the groves of the engraving.

"Can I open it?"

Rose nodded.

Jane's little fingers worked at the locket until it opened stiffly. Inside was a lock of thick, jet-black hair.

"A little piece of your father for you to carry with you," Rose said, her voice thick with emotion. She took the chain and slipped it over her daughter's head, tucking it beneath her shift. The metal felt cold against Jane's skin.

"But this is yours. Father gave it to you," Jane objected.

"And now I'm giving it to you. As an early Christmas present." Her mother gripped her shoulders. "You must keep this hidden always. Never tell anyone you have it. Do you understand?"

Jane nodded.

"Good girl. Now, put your cloak on."

"Where are we going?"

But Rose didn't answer. She climbed slowly to her feet and buttoned on her own cloak. She slung the duffel bag over her shoulder and reached for Jane's hand. As they made their way towards the door, the last candle in the room hissed and gutted, plunging their home into blackness. Another home, Jane was sure, she would never see again.

CHAPTER 2

Jane and her mother trudged through street after street lined with stained, grey snow. The fresh snowfall had not made it to Whitechapel and what was left on the ground was grey and slushy in parts, icy in others. Jane's legs ached. She had been on her feet all day. She clung tightly to her mother's hand as they made their way through the slum. The narrow streets were crammed with people; some clustered-on street corners, others with their heads down, walking quickly as though they could not wait to leave the place. A fire burned inside an old metal barrel, casting a flickering orange light over the street.

Jane felt eyes on her. She touched the small

bulge at her chest where the locket was hidden beneath her clothes. She pressed herself against her mother's side.

They stopped outside a large stone building. Jane stared up at its looming black iron gates. A sudden wave of fear shot through her. "Where are we?" she dared to ask.

"The Workhouse. We're to stay here a little while," Rose managed, a tremor in her voice. Suddenly, her breath left her as she doubled over, clutching at her stomach. Her hand tightened around Jane's.

"Mama? Are you all right?" Jane felt tears stab her throat.

Rose straightened. She drew in a long breath. "I'm fine, darling. Everything's going to be all right. But you must be brave now. Promise me you will be brave."

Jane nodded, unable to speak in case the tears that were threatening spilt down her cheeks. She followed her mother up to the large wooden door. Rose knocked loudly.

"We are in need of shelter," she said when a woman in a white uniform opened the door.

The woman glanced at Rose's swollen stomach, "Yes, I'm sure you are. Come inside then." Her tone was flat and unfriendly. Jane and Rose followed the woman down a long grey corridor. She gestured to a wooden bench against one wall. "Wait here. I'll find out if the workhouse master can see you."

Rose nodded her thanks. She sat on the bench and pulled Jane down beside her, cupping her daughter's hand in both of hers. Jane sat close to her mother, pressing her eyes against her arm. She shivered back a mix of fear and cold.

After a few moments, the woman in the white uniform returned with a frown on her face as though it was all too much trouble. "Follow me."

They were led into an office at the end of the passage. It was colourless and bare like the corridor. The workhouse master sat behind a large wooden desk, his eyes almost hidden beneath thick grey eyebrows. The flickering lamp caused grotesque shadows to dance across the room. Jane felt tears threaten behind her eyes.

"Name?" the workhouse master barked.

"Walker," Rose managed. "Rose Walker. And my daughter, Jane."

"Age?"

"My daughter is seven."

The master scrawled down their details. He peered at them as though they were insects. His gaze lingered on Rose's swollen belly. "I can see the situation is somewhat urgent."

Rose coughed, "Yes, sir. Most urgent."

"No husband I presume?"

"I'm a widow, sir, He'll never see this child," she patted her stomach and hoped she had made it clear that the child had been conceived in lawful wedlock.

The master nodded, "The board will not be meeting over Christmas so there will be no need to face them." There was weariness in his voice, along with more than a little disgust. "In their absence, I will admit you myself. You are clearly in need."

Rose nodded, "Thank you, sir. Thank you very much."

Jane stared up at her mother. Surely they were not to stay here? Not in this cold, colourless place with these cold, unfriendly people?

"I don't want to stay here, Mama," she whispered. "I want to go home. Please can't we just go home?"

Rose pressed her hands to her daughter's shoulders and spoke with a firmness Jane had never heard before, "Listen to me, my darling. I wish we could go home, too. But there is not enough money to pay Mr Branston the rent this month. So, we cannot stay in our room. I'm sorry." Rose's voice wavered, "Do you understand?"

Scared by her mother's new bluntness, Jane managed a nod.

Rose's strained smile returned. "Good girl." She reached out and squeezed her daughter's hand in hers. She looked down at her, tears welling behind her eyes. "It's time to be brave now, Jane. Promise me you will be brave."

CHAPTER 3

Rhythmic footsteps sounded down the dimly lit passage. Into the office came a large woman in a similar uniform to the lady who had let them inside. Her steel grey hair was tucked beneath a cap, her face lined and shadowy. She looked down at Jane with cold, flinty eyes. "Come with me, child."

Jane glanced desperately at Rose.

I want to stay with my mother, she longed to say, but the nurse's icy gaze and her mother's firm words had stolen her voice. Instead, she just nodded. Rose gave her hand a final squeeze. As Jane glanced over her shoulder at her mother, she was sure she could see tears spilling down her cheeks. Jane felt a stabbing in her own throat but she had promised her mother she would be brave. And so brave she would be.

The nurse led her down the passage to a room finished with murky white tiles. Three tubs were lined up in the middle of the floor. The nurse nodded at one of the baths. A thin layer of dirty water sat at the bottom. "In," she told Jane.

Too afraid to argue, Jane edged her way towards the bathtub. She thought of the locket around her neck containing the lock of her father's hair. She had promised her mother she would keep it hidden. Turning away from the nurse, she unlaced her cloak and pulled it from her shoulders, sliding the locket from around her neck as she did so. Keeping it clenched tightly in her fist, she removed her dress and underclothes, her thin arms trying to cover her nakedness.

The nurse looked unfazed. "In," she said again.

The water was icy. It stole Jane's breath; the shock of it caused her fingers to clench tighter around the locket.

"Wash yourself," the nurse barked, pointing to the soap. "You'll no doubt be carrying all manner of filth coming in off the streets."

She wanted to say that she didn't live on the streets and that she washed herself each morning. Even after they had moved to the tenement, Rose ensured that her daughter was kept clean and presentable.

Jane decided to keep silent and soaped herself obediently, then scrambled from the bathtub. She stood shivering, water running from her skin onto the tiles. The nurse thrust an armful of clothes at Jane. "Put these on, child."

Jane dried herself hurriedly and climbed into the fresh underclothes, slipping the locket over her head. She pulled on the white dress and apron. The clothes were scratchy against her skin. She tried not to wriggle and show her discomfort, sensing the nurse would not be pleased by it.

The nurse nodded to the cloth cap in Jane's hand. "And the hat," she clicked her tongue against the roof of her mouth.

Obediently, Jane pulled it on over her wet hair. The nurse gave a faint nod of approval, then led her out of the bathroom and down another gloomy hallway. Jane could hear the faint chatter of children's voices.

She stopped walking. "What about Emily?"

The nurse stopped her relentless, confused. "Who is Emily?"

"My doll. I have her with me every night. My Mama packed her in the bag she brought."

The nurse shook her head. "Not here. She will be returned to you on your departure."

Jane looked as if she were about to burst into tears.

The nurse sighed and softened her tone. "She will be quite safe. I will see to it myself. Now come."

Jane dared not retort and so followed in her wake.

The nurse swung a heavy door open and lit the lamp to reveal a room lined with narrow beds. Arms and legs spilt out of each of them. There were at least two girls in each bed, Jane noticed. Most held three or four. Some of the children were sleeping, some whispering, others squinting in the imposing light. The nurse pointed to the bed closest to the window. Two other girls lay in it, their bodies stiff and frozen at the sight of the nurse.

"In there," she ordered.

Jane hesitated. How was she to fit in the bed with the other two girls? She had thought the sleeping pallet she had shared with her mother in the apartment was cramped, but in comparison to this bed, it seemed enormous. Too afraid to argue, she pulled off her dress and shoes and slid into bed with the two girls. She felt an elbow in her spine but said nothing.

And then the room was plunged into darkness and the nurse was gone.

The girl beside Jane in the bed turned to whisper in her ear. "There's no room for you here," she hissed. "You're in my space."

Jane shuffled to the very edge of the bed and clung to the mattress to stop herself from falling out. Then she closed her eyes and cried herself to sleep.

JANE WAS WOKEN by the elbow digging into her spine. Yanked out of her dreams, she leapt from the bed, whirling around to see who had delivered the blow. An older girl glared at her from the edge of the mattress. Her hair was dark, her eyes hard and unfriendly.

"You're in my space, you useless fool," she hissed.

Unsure what to say, Jane just stared at her, her

mouth hanging open. She had never come across someone so nasty before.

"What's the matter?" the girl drawled, "don't you know how to speak?"

From a bed on the other side of the room, Jane heard a fit of giggles.

"Leave her alone, Elsie," said an older girl. "She's new."

Elsie snorted, "Don't I know it? She kept me up all night bawling." Her foot stuck out from beneath the blankets and jabbed Jane in the hip. "What's the matter, girl? You missing your mother? Do you even have one?"

At the mention of her mother, Jane's chest tightened. She said nothing. She knew she could not cry in front of these girls ever again.

A bell sounded suddenly, making the girls groan. Jane watched dumbly as they filed out of bed.

"Don't just stand there, fool," Elsie hissed at her. "Get yourself dressed or the matron will have her cane out."

Jane swallowed heavily and snatched her uniform from the end of the bed. Soon, she was following the other girls into the dining hall. They were seated at long wooden tables, bowls of gruel set in front of them.

Jane had never seen so many children in one place in her life. There must be hundreds of children here, she thought. Some were older than her, others seemed barely old enough to walk. All of them were girls, she noticed. All dressed in the same white uniform as her. All with their hair tucked beneath a stiff white cap. There must be boys here too, Jane thought. She wondered distantly where they were. There was no room in the hall for any more children. Perhaps they were kept in another part of the workhouse.

None of the girls spoke. The matron and two nurses walked up and down the hall, their footsteps echoing rhythmically on the flagstones.

Jane stared at the grey mess in her bowl. Her stomach turned over. She had no appetite. All she wanted was to see her mother. Where was she? What was she doing? No one had told her anything about where she was or when Jane might see her again. She was desperate to ask but too afraid of the nurses with their cold eyes. She could feel her tears threatening to return. She blinked them away hurriedly. Crying in this place, she was sure, would do her no good.

When the nurses weren't looking, Elsie leant across the table and hissed at Jane. "Give me your food, fool. I'm hungry."

Jane swallowed heavily. She didn't want the gruel but the coldness in the older girl's eyes scared her. She pushed her bowl across the table towards her. Elsie emptied its congealing contents into her own dish and handed it back to Jane without a word.

After breakfast, it was time for lessons.

The matron sought Jane out across the hall. "You," she said, "you know your letters?"

"Yes, ma'am," Jane managed, her voice stuck in her throat. "I know a little."

The matron nodded towards Elsie and the other older girls. "Then you'll go with them."

Jane's stomach tightened. She wished she had pretended she was unable to read. Wished she had been sent to lessons with the little children.

The matron clicked her tongue against her teeth, "Well don't just stand here, child. I told you to go with them."

Jane hurried across the hall to where the group of girls was disappearing into the corridor. Elsie gave a cold chuckle when she saw her, "I think you're in the wrong class, you stupid fool. This is for big girls who don't cry for their mothers." The other girls howled with laughter.

The nurse leading them towards their classroom looked over her shoulder, giving Elsie an icy stare, "That's quite enough, Miss Cook."

Elsie said no more but the sneer on her face remained. Jane stared at her feet until they reached the classroom.

When lessons had finished, the girls were sent to the kitchen. Jane was led to a bench piled with a mountain of potatoes. A woman in uniform similar to her own handed her a knife.

"Peel and cut them," she said shortly.

Jane stared at the pile, "All of them?"

"All of them."

The woman seemed to catch Jane's bewildered expression, "You got to earn your bed somehow, don't you? We all do. I'm sure they can find a job breaking rocks for you if you don't fancy peeling potatoes."

Obediently, Jane took the first potato and began to peel. She had peeled potatoes only once before. She was slow and uncertain. The blade seemed to dart uncontrollably in her hand. She frowned with concentration.

After an hour, she had managed just eight potatoes. She could hear the other girls giggling from across the kitchen.

"She'll be here til Christmas," Elsie laughed.

Another girl snorted, "She'll be here til *next* Christmas."

Gritting her teeth, Jane picked up the next potato. The girls were right, she was far too slow. She tried to peel faster. The blade shot out uncontrollably, slicing her finger. She bit her lip, determined not to cry out. Blood beaded on her skin. She put her finger in her mouth and sucked, her eyes watering from the pain. Behind her, the older girls roared with laughter.

CHAPTER 4

Christmas Day, Jane thought when she opened her eyes. A day she had always loved.

But this morning she felt nothing but heaviness in her chest. All she wanted to do was lie in bed and cry. But of course, there was to be no such thing in the workhouse. She wanted Mama.

When the bell sounded, she climbed out of bed with the other girls and climbed dutifully into her uniform. Was she to spend her Christmas Day peeling potatoes?

But there was to be no work that day, Jane learned as they ate their breakfast of gruel. A morning of reading, then a church service, followed by Christmas Dinner.

As she realised she would not have to sit in lessons with Elsie and the other girls that day, Jane felt a faint flicker of happiness. Perhaps this day might not be so dreadful, she thought, if only she could see her mother. How she wanted to ask about her; ask if she might see her, if only to wish her a happy Christmas. But the hardness in the nurses' eyes made her chest tighten in fear.

THEY CROWDED into the workhouse chapel. The room was full of people, all the girls and some boys as well. Jane's heart leapt when she saw a group of women being led into the room, all wearing similar uniforms to her own. She tried to glance around the church for her mother. She couldn't see her among the sea of bodies. Hit with a fresh pang of loneliness, she pressed a hand to where the locket lay against her chest.

Mama, she thought, *where are you?*

WITH THE CHURCH SERVICE FINISHED, the girls were herded back towards the dining hall. The tables were lined with plates and sprigs of holly hung over the doors. Jane felt an ache in her chest. How she longed to be out in on the well-to-do streets of London, her arms full of holly and early snowdrops.

Lilies.

Bluebells

Roses.

How she longed to be back in that tiny cold room, huddled up beside her mother. How she longed to be anywhere but here.

The girls filed to the tables and sat. Elsie and the other girls giggled and chattered, ignoring Jane.

Good. She did not want to speak to any of them. She did not want to speak to anyone but her mother.

Plates were set in front of them, a lavish Christmas dinner of roast beef and vegetables. She was surprised at such fare being served, even if it was Christmas day. Jane stared at the food. It had been a long time since she had eaten meat, but the workhouse had stolen her appetite. Around her, she could hear Elsie and the other girls talking loudly. She kept her eyes down, not wanting to look at them.

She glanced up at the sound of footsteps. *Click,*

click. Jane recognised the sound of the nurse's footsteps.

"Jane Walker," she said, "have you finished eating?"

Her heart began to race suddenly at being singled out by the nurse. She managed a nod. "Yes, ma'am."

The nurse looked at her untouched plate but did not comment. "Come with me, please. The matron wishes to see you."

Jane's stomach turned over. Had she done something wrong? Made a mistake somehow? Perhaps Elsie had been telling stories about how she was such a slow worker. Perhaps they had heard how she had taken an hour to peel eight potatoes and then cut her finger open… She clasped her hand into a fist so that no one could see the cut.

"Quickly now," said the nurse. Jane stood hurriedly, ignoring the whispers of the other girls. She heard the nurse say: "Quiet now, Elsie," but she didn't look back at her.

She followed the nurse down the gloomy hall towards an office similar to that of the workhouse master.

"Jane Walker," said the matron when the nurse

ushered her inside. She was sitting behind a desk the way the master had been when she and her mother had arrived. She twisted anxiously at her apron.

"Yes, ma'am?" her voice was tiny.

"I'm afraid I have some bad news."

The churning in Jane's stomach intensified.

"Your mother gave birth early this morning. I'm sorry to say she did not survive."

Jane stared at the woman. She felt cold, then suddenly hot. The world began to swim around her. She clutched at the edge of the desk to keep her balance.

Her mother dead? No. Surely not. This had to be some kind of cruel joke. It just had to be. Her mother was all she had in the whole world. There was no way she would have left her alone in this place. "No," she said. "No, you're wrong. My mama isn't dead."

"I'm sorry, child," said the matron, a tiny flicker of sympathy softening her steely voice.

Jane tried to reply but could find no words. Her throat tightened with tears.

"I assume you have no relatives you can go to?"

She shook her head. "No, ma'am," she managed.

"Then you will stay here until you are of age." The matron nodded to the nurse. "Take her."

And back down the hall, Jane went, trailing the nurse back towards the dining hall.

"No," she managed. "Please. I just want to go to bed."

The nurse sighed, tilting her grey head in consideration. Finally, she sighed, "Very well then. Just this once."

Alone in the sleeping quarters, Jane crawled into the bed and squeezed herself into a ball as the tears she had been holding back spilt violently down her cheeks.

Her world had changed once again.

Her father dead.

Her mother dead.

She realised that she was an orphan, with not a living soul to care for her.

It was Christmas.

She was a Christmas orphan.

It was now a day she would hate forever.

She sobbed into the mattress until, gripped by exhaustion, she finally fell asleep.

CHAPTER 5

Without her mother, life at the workhouse became unbearable. She soon realised that girls with mothers or fathers were allowed to see them for one hour each day. This was after a weeklong settling-in period of forced separation. Now that she was an orphan, Jane didn't get that pleasure.

Jane would sleep each night on the edge of the mattress, Elsie's elbows digging into her back. The bullies would taunt her endlessly throughout their lessons and chores and force her to give them her gruel.

Jane couldn't remember the last time she had not been hungry or tired. All that brought her solace was the feel of the locket against her chest.

Her mother's locket, clutching a strand of her father's dark hair. It was all she had of her family now. The only thing in the world that did not make her feel completely alone.

And then one day as she leant forward to clean the inside of one of the stoves in the kitchens, the locket slipped out from beneath her pinafore. She tried hurriedly to shove it back beneath her shift before anyone noticed.

She felt a hand on her arm. "What you got there, little fool?" one of the older girls was grinning at her with a threatening, unfriendly smile. Elsie and two of the other girls came towards them.

"It's nothing," Jane said hurriedly, her heart beginning to race. She looked desperately around the room for the matron or nurses, but they were nowhere to be seen.

"Didn't look like nothing."

Anger gripped her suddenly, "I said it's nothing." She tried to pull away. "Leave me alone."

Two of the girls grabbed her arms.

"Let go of me!" Jane cried.

Elsie reached beneath her pinafore and snatched the locket, pulling it roughly over Jane's head. The girls crowded around, peering at the gold jewellery.

"Give it back!" Jane shrieked.

Elsie laughed, holding it out in front of her. "Come and get it."

Jane felt rage build inside her, hot and uncontrollable. Elsie fumbled with the locket, trying to open it. No. Jane would not, *could not*, let that awful girl get her hands on that precious lock of hair. She snatched the fire poker from beside the hearth and swung wildly. Elsie and the other girls leapt backwards and the locket spilt to the hearth. Jane dived after it, the fire poker clattering to the floor. She felt someone grab a fistful of her hair. Her arms flailed wildly, the anger that had been stirring in her for the past six months finally tearing itself free.

"Enough!" The girls froze at the sound of the matron's booming voice. Her footsteps click-clacked their way towards them. Jane stared up at the woman from her sprawl on the floor, her eyes hard and unrepentant. The other girls parted, allowing the matron to approach Jane.

"Stand up, Jane Walker."

Jane stood slowly, the locket in her fist.

"What is that in your hand?"

"Nothing."

"Don't lie to me!" the matron boomed. "Show me what's in your hand."

Jane swallowed heavily, her anger beginning to give way to fear. She opened her fist, gulping down her tears when the matron took the locket from her hand. The woman's eyes passed over the other girls, "Get back to work." She glared fiercely at Jane. "Jane Walker, you will come with me."

There was silence as Jane followed the matron from the room. Not even Elsie dared to whisper.

THE MATRON STRODE down the grey corridor and unlocked a room Jane had never seen before. It was white and bare, with nothing inside but a thin mattress and a crude enamel-chipped metal chamber pot.

"Inside," the matron ordered.

Jane's palms prickled with sweat. She stepped inside the tiny room, her terror making her both hot and cold at once.

"You will stay in here for a time and think about your behaviour," the matron said sharply. "There is no place for violence in this institution, Miss Walker. The Parish of Whitechapel has provided you with Christian charity. You will do well to remember that. We are not animals."

Jane shivered. Inside was so cold her breath plumed out in front of her. She blinked away her tears. "Please ma'am, may I have my locket?" She knew it was bold of her to ask but the thought of being trapped in this tiny cell without the reminder of her parents was too awful to bear.

"I will keep hold of the locket," the matron said firmly. "It will be returned to you on your release."

"On my release from this cell?" Jane dared to ask.

The matron made a noise from the back of her throat. "On your release from the workhouse. When you are of age."

Jane's tears spilt suddenly. "Please, ma'am," she begged, "it's all I have of my mother and father. I—"

Her words were cut off by the slamming of the door. Engulfed in grey gloom, Jane curled up on the mattress and cried.

CHAPTER 6

For two days, Jane sat alone in the dark, her knees pulled to her chest. Anger bubbled inside her along with an ache of grief. She missed her mother. Her father. She missed their house by the park with the beautiful garden. She missed going out into the streets with an armful of flowers.

Missed selling lilies and bluebells and roses of every colour.

Her mind flickered suddenly to Mrs Cron, her favourite customer.

Aren't you a clever girl? One day, I'm going to steal you and you'll come and work for me.

Jane straightened. Yes, she thought. She was a

clever girl. She could work in Mrs Cron's kitchen, in that big house where the kindly woman cooked and cleaned for the wealthy family who lived behind the square. Jane felt suddenly alive with determination.

In the morning, the door creaked open. "Come on then, Jane Walker," said the matron. "Out. Go and eat your breakfast with the other girls."

Jane walked out of solitary and down the grey corridor. She kept walking past the dining hall, past the workhouse master's office and out the big wooden door and into the street.

It was that simple.

No one stopped her. No one came after her. She looked back over her shoulder at the looming building. Then she turned away. And she walked quicker.

She hurried through the streets of Whitechapel with her eyes on her feet, glancing up only to check her bearings. She knew these streets, had walked them many times with flowers in her arms. She walked the same route now; out of the east end, past Saint Paul's and into the square where she had stood selling flowers.

Jane hovered on the edge of the square. Mrs Cron had come this way each time Jane had seen her, through the square on her way back from the market, her basket packed with meat and vegetables.

She waited, praying that Mrs Cron would be visiting the market today. Several people turned to look at her and she remembered she was still wearing her scratchy workhouse uniform. Self-consciously, she pulled off the cap and tossed it into the street.

She waited in the square all day, watching the sea of strangers come and go, watching all the faces that weren't Mrs Cron.

The sun was beginning to sink. Jane felt disappointment and fear well inside her. Dare she return to the workhouse? They would punish her again for running away, surely. She'd be forced to spend another day or more in that cell. She thought of Elsie and the other girls, their leering faces and bitter taunts. No, Jane thought bitterly, she would not go back to the workhouse. Not ever. She would rather sleep on the street.

She looked around for shelter. If she stayed close to the square, she could come back in the morning and wait for Mrs Cron.

But just as Jane was about to leave, she caught sight of a large woman in a black housemaid's uniform, a basket clutched to her chest. Her heart skipped. Mrs Cron! Jane ran towards her, a grin spreading across her face.

The woman started at the sight of a child racing towards her. She pressed a hand to her heaving chest. "Goodness, girl, you gave me such a fright barrelling up to me like that!" She reached into the pocket of her cloak and pulled out a penny, "Here. Take this and be on your way now. That's a good girl."

Jane gulped down her breath, "Mrs Cron, it's me, Jane Walker."

The old woman frowned.

"I used to sell you flowers right here. Do you remember? I knew all the names of all the flowers. Roses and bluebells and Lilies. Holly and snowdrops in the winter. You said I was a clever girl."

Mrs Cron's eyebrows shot up as recognition registered on her faintly lined face. "Goodness me. Yes of course." She looked up and down at Jane's stained workhouse uniform. "I wondered what had happened to you, my girl. I came to buy flowers one day and you weren't there." She put a soft hand on the top of Jane's head. At the gentle touch, her tears spilt suddenly.

"My mother is dead," she coughed. "And my father. I can't go back to the workhouse. I just can't. The girls all hate me, and I'll be punished for running away and... and...."

Mrs Cron pulled her into her arms, "There, there child. It's all right now."

Jane clung to the woman's vast middle, "You said one day I could come and work for you. Help you in your kitchen in the big house."

Mrs Cron stepped back, holding Jane at arm's length, "Of course, little one. Of course you can come with me."

MRS CRON LIVED in an enormous white house two blocks from the square. There were more windows and chimneys than Jane could count. The house seemed to stretch endlessly upwards towards the cloudy sky.

She followed the old woman through the servant's entrance and into a large kitchen. It smelled of roast meat and herbs, making Jane's stomach groan loudly.

Mrs Cron smiled, "Sit down, child. I'll fetch you some supper."

Jane's mouth began to water. She'd not eaten all day. Mrs Cron set a large bowl of stew in front of her and Jane began to spoon it hungrily into her mouth. It was thick with meat and vegetables. Jane could not remember the last time she'd eaten anything that had tasted so good.

Mrs Cron chuckled, "Slow down, little one. You'll give yourself a dreadful stomach ache."

Jane emptied her bowl and Mrs Cron spooned another ladle of stew into it. Jane grinned and continued eating.

The housekeeper sat opposite her at the table. "Now then. Tell me what they've had you do in that workhouse. Cleaning and sewing? Can you cook?"

Jane nodded, "I can clean and sew, ma'am. But I've never cooked before. Only peeled vegetables. I can learn, though. I promise. If you let me stay, I promise I'll be the fastest learner you ever saw."

Mrs Cron reached out and placed her soft hand over Jane's. "If it were up to me, child, I'd have you stay in a second. But we need to ask Mr Weir. He's the man who owns the house, you see. The master. The man who does the hiring."

Jane's stomach twisted, her thoughts leaping back to their meeting with the workhouse master the night she and her mother had come in off the street. She pushed her bowl away, her appetite suddenly gone. As though sensing her fear, Mrs Cron smiled warmly.

"It's all right, child. There's nothing to be afraid of." She stood and held out her hand, "Come on then. Shall we go and see him?"

Mrs Cron led Jane through the big house, winding up a large staircase and down a hallway. She knocked on one of the doors.

"Excuse me, Mr Weir, may I have a moment of your time?"

A man grunted from behind the door. "Come in, Mrs Cron," he said gruffly. Clutching Jane's hand, the housekeeper pushed open the door and entered what looked to be a man's study. Mr Weir stood in front of his desk, arms folded across his chest. He was a tall man with wide shoulders and a creased forehead. He peered down at Jane as though she were an insect. His eyes were grey like his hair and had the same steeliness behind them as the matron's. Jane felt the muscles in her shoulders tighten. She clung a little tighter to Mrs Cron's hand.

"And who is this?" Mr Weir asked.

"Her name is Jane Walker, sir. An orphan. I thought I might use her in the house. If it pleases you, of course."

Mr Weir raised his furry eyebrows. He peered at Jane's stained white uniform. "She has run from the workhouse?"

"She has, sir. In Whitechapel. And I'm sure you cannot blame her. She'll do far better here, I know it."

"And since when have you made a habit of plucking children from the streets, Mrs Cron?"

Jane stiffened. She listened edgily as Mrs Cron relayed the story of her flower selling and the way she had waited for the woman on the edge of the square.

"I see," said Weir when Mrs Cron had stopped talking.

"Please, sir, have a heart. The poor girl has just lost her mother."

Weir rubbed his chin, "She's a runaway."

Mrs Cron snorted, "You really think the union will miss one child out of two thousand? You'll be doing them a favour by taking her off their hands."

"What of her uniform? It's stolen property." He began to pace.

Jane's heart pounded. He was going to send her back to the workhouse, she was sure of it. She'd been thrown back into solitary for running away and then shoved back into that bed to contend with Elsie's elbows.

But then Mr Weir said, "Very well." He pinned Jane with charcoal eyes. "The girl can stay under your care, Mrs Cron. But I will return to the workhouse tomorrow to buy her. I do not want any illegal runaways under my roof."

Despite the man's cold demeanour, Jane felt a great wave of relief rush over her. She grinned up at Mrs Cron. "Thank you," she gushed.

Mrs Cron pressed a soft hand to her shoulder. "It's not me you ought to be thanking, child. It's your new master."

Jane turned nervously to face Mr Weir. He looked down at her expectantly. She felt his gaze searing into her. She shifted uncomfortably. "Thank you, sir," she managed. "Thank you ever so much."

He nodded, "I'll need to return your uniform." He turned to Mrs Cron, "Do you have something the girl might wear?"

"I'm sure we can find something, sir."

Jane looked up at the housekeeper to see her smiling warmly. But she could feel Mr Weir's cold eyes on her and tried to ignore the shiver they sent coursing through her body.

CHAPTER 7

Jane woke early the next morning, determined to prove herself a good assistant to Mrs Cron. She was determined not to be sent back to the workhouse.

She showed Mrs Cron all she had learned in the kitchens in Whitechapel; peeling and cutting vegetables, boiling bones to make broth, and showed her the way she could empty the fire grates and blacken the hearths.

"Very good, child," said the housekeeper, making Jane's insides warm. "Now I'm going to teach you how to bake a loaf of bread."

As they were finishing kneading the dough, Mr Weir came to the kitchen with a bundle of clothing in his arms. He nodded to Jane to join him. She did, cautiously. Mrs Cron watched them from beside the range.

"I've purchased you from the workhouse as an apprentice to Mrs Cron here," Mr Weir told her. "You're my responsibility now. My worker."

Jane nodded.

"I expect you to behave appropriately. Remember your place."

"Yes, sir. Of course, sir." She tried to push the tremor of fear from her voice.

"Good." Mr Weir held out the bundle of clothing. "They gave me these to return to you."

Jane glanced down at them, a lump forming in her throat. In her arms was the clothing she had been wearing on the day they entered the workhouse. There were other pieces from her mother's bag as well. Some of her clothes and some of her mother's. And on top of them all was Emily, her beloved doll.

"Thank you," Jane managed, blinking away her tears. Then she began to worry. "Sir? Was there perhaps a locket? My mother gave it to me just before we went to the workhouse."

Mr Weir frowned. "No, child. That is your share, I am told."

Her heart almost burst with pain. She did not

think about the precious locket when she walked out of the workhouse. Now it was lost for good. More than likely the matron had pocketed it for herself to sell at the pawnshop.

"May I take this to my room?" she asked Mr Weir in a tiny voice.

He nodded, "Quickly. And then you will return to the kitchen and continue your chores."

Obediently, Jane ran down to the servant's quarters and let herself into her bedroom as the tears spilt down her cheeks. She held her mother's clothing to her, sobbing silently into the worn wool. She could still smell her mother's warm, musky scent. She placed Emily on her bed, leaning against her pillow. Tonight, she would sleep with her.

A knock at the door made her start. Mrs Cron's capped head appeared around the door. "Can I come in, child?"

Jane nodded tearfully.

"Those were your mother's things?" she asked pointing at the pile of clothing.

"Some of them."

"And the doll was yours, obviously."

"Yes. Her name is Emily. My parents gave it to me for Christmas two years ago."

"Oh, my little one," Mrs Cron pulled her into her arms and squeezed tightly. "It's all right. You cry if you need to. Let it out."

And so Jane stood with her arms around Mrs Cron's middle and sobbed the way she had wanted to do for months. When her tears finally stopped, she felt exhausted but better. "Does Mr Weir really own me now?"

Mrs Cron smiled, "Sort of. You are now an apprentice. He's paid money so that you can work for him here in the household. But when you reach eighteen, you can stay or leave as you like, assuming the master wants you to stay, that is. Do you understand?"

Jane smiled unconvincingly, "Yes, I do."

Mrs Cron pushed Jane's straggly red hair off her wet cheeks. "Come on now," she said, "I've something else for you to do. Something I think you might like."

Jane wiped away the last of her tears. "What is it?"

Mrs Cron held out her hand. "Come with me."

Out they went into the expansive garden behind the house. At once, Jane felt lighter, her heart quickening with joy as they wove through the trees. Needles of sunlight shone through the leaves, warming Jane's cheeks.

They stopped beside a garden bed overgrown with flowers and tangled vines. Bumblebees hummed and circled. Despite its wildness, the garden was the loveliest thing Jane had ever seen. She inhaled deeply, drawing in the powerful floral smell.

Mrs Cron caught her grin. "Yes, I thought you might like it out here. Mr Jacob is the gardener here. He does a fine job of the lawns, but he's let this place grow out of control. Perhaps you might like to look after it?"

Jane's smile widened, "Oh yes, please, Mrs Cron! I would love to!"

The housekeeper smiled, "Good. We've work to do in the house this afternoon but you can have an hour out here. I'll come and fetch you when it's time to come in."

Jane nodded. "Thank you," she gushed, "thank you so much!"

Mrs Cron pressed a warm hand to Jane's shoulder and disappeared into the house.

Jane stood on the edge of the garden bed, surveying the tangle of greenery. Weeds were growing between the flowers, threatening to overtake the plot.

Removing them would be her first job, she decided.

She got to work digging out the weeds, singing to herself as she did. How lovely it was to feel the earth on her hands again. How lovely to be surrounded by such beautiful scents. She felt suddenly happily close to her mother.

"What are you doing?"

The voice made Jane start. She leapt to her feet and whirled around to see a young boy standing on the edge of the garden bed. He looked no more than a year or two older than her, a sweep of brown hair hanging over one eye. Jane could tell by his neat blue trousers and waistcoat that he was not a servant like her.

"I'm sorry," she spluttered, scrambling to her feet and dusting the dirt from her apron. "Mrs Cron, she said I could tidy the garden and I thought to get the weeds out and, and—"

The boy's face lit suddenly with a warm smile. A faint dimple appeared in one cheek. "It's all right," he said. "You're doing a fine job."

Jane began to relax a little. "Really?"

The boy nodded, "This garden was such a mess

last time I saw it." He pointed at a carpet of pink and yellow flowers Jane had uncovered. "I never saw those ones before."

"It's honeysuckle. One of the signs that spring is on the way," she said. "They were hiding under the weeds. They'll grow bigger now the sun can reach them." She touched one of the petals gently. "Don't they have the most interesting flowers?"

The boy nodded, "They smell good, too. This whole garden does." He eyed Jane curiously. "You know a lot about flowers."

She gave a small smile.

"Who are you?" he asked, curiously, but kindly.

"Jane. Jane Walker. I'm to help Mrs Cron around the house. I'm her new apprentice."

"You're to stay with us?"

She nodded, unsure if the boy saw this as a good or a bad thing.

"My name is Daniel," he told her. "Daniel Weir."

"You're the master's son," she said in a small voice.

Daniel nodded and Jane felt something sink inside her. She knew well that the master's children did not spend their time with the help. But Daniel gave another warm smile.

"What else do you know about the flowers?" he asked.

"Lots of things." Jane lifted her chin proudly. "I know the best time to plant the different types. And how much sun they need. And the names of them all..." She faded out, suddenly aware of sounding boastful.

"How do you know so much about these things?" Daniel asked.

"My mother loved flowers," she said, a sudden wave of grief overwhelming her. She swallowed heavily, determined not to cry in front of the master's son. "She taught me all about them. I used to sell them in the street. That's how I met Mrs Cron."

"Where is your mother now?" Daniel asked.

"Dead." Jane looked at her feet.

For a moment, Daniel didn't reply. Then he said: "My mother loved flowers, too. This was her garden."

Jane met his eyes. "Your mother is dead too?"

He nodded, "She died three years ago. Influenza." He tilted his head, his eyes fixed on the patch of honeysuckle Jane had uncovered. "This garden has been overgrown ever since. I'm glad you're going to care for it now."

Jane wound her apron around her fingers. "Did you ever stop being sad after she died?" she asked after a moment. "Did you ever stop wanting to cry?"

Daniel frowned as though considering her question. "I know I will always miss her. But I don't want to cry every day anymore. At first, I did. But every day it got a little easier. It's much better now," he gave her a reassuring smile that Jane tried to return.

He looked back at the garden. "May I help?"

"You want to help with my chores?"

Daniel shrugged, "It looks like fun."

Jane grinned, "Of course you can help. Just make sure you only pull out the weeds."

CHAPTER 8

*E*ach afternoon when the chores were done, Jane and Daniel met in the gardens to work on his mother's old garden bed. They had cleared the plot of its weeds and trimmed the tufty grass that had begun to grow around the edges. Freshly exposed to the late winter sunshine, the garden had flourished, and wild bursts of colour exploded among the greenery as spring arrived.

Daniel had other things to show her too; the trees he liked to climb and the foxhole at the bottom of the garden.

When the weather began to turn, they took to sitting by the fire in the parlour; Daniel helping Jane with her letters. Together, they would read his favourite books out loud, Jane forming the words slowly and carefully, Daniel assisting her with the words she didn't know.

Jane had always loved to read but her lessons at the workhouse had filled her with dread. What a joy it was to have Daniel's warm, patient voice guiding her through the books instead of Elsie leering over her shoulder.

One rainy day in March, they were halfway through *The South Sea Whaler* when Mr Weir strode into the room. The two children leapt to their feet, Jane bobbing a hurried curtsey. She felt Mr Weir's cold eyes on her. "Out of here, girl. I'm sure Mrs Cron has something better for you to do with your time than bother my son."

She scurried out of the room, Daniel staring after her as she left. But curiosity prevented her from leaving. She stood outside the parlour, her ear pressed to the door.

"What have I told you about spending time with that girl?" Mr Weir boomed.

"But Father, I—"

"She came from the streets, Daniel. We know nothing about her. How many times must I remind you of that?"

"I don't understand why that matters, Father."

"It matters because of who you are. It matters

because of the family you're a part of. I have spent my life building the business that you will inherit. You will not sully our good name by spending your time with street urchins like that girl."

"Jane is my friend," Daniel said defiantly. "I don't care where she comes from."

Mr Weir's anger exploded suddenly, shouting a stream of angry words at his son.

Impertinent. Disrespectful. Far too bold.

Jane felt a fresh flush of anger at the man.

If Daniel replied to his father's outburst, she did not hear it. Footsteps came towards the door and Jane disappeared hurriedly towards the kitchen.

"Mr Weir doesn't want me to be friends with Daniel," Jane told Mrs Cron the next day as they walked towards the market.

Mrs Cron made a noise from the back of her throat. "I know, my love." She put a consoling hand on Jane's shoulder.

"It's because I'm just a girl from the workhouse," she said sadly. "Because I'm nothing but a housemaid. He thinks I'm not good enough for Daniel to spend time with. We weren't even doing anything bad. Just reading books and playing in the garden."

Mrs Cron didn't reply.

Jane sniffed. "It isn't fair."

The woman rubbed her shoulder. "I know isn't, my love. But I'm afraid that's just the way the world works. There's not a thing you or I can do about it." She caught Jane's eye. "Don't you forget now, you owe the master a great deal. Imagine where you'd be if it weren't for him."

Jane nodded acceptingly. "I know." Her voice was tiny.

Mrs Cron pointed towards the market. "Look now. This will cheer you up, I'm sure."

Jane let out a cry of delight. On the edge of the market stood the first flower seller of the spring. Roses and bluebells exploded from the stall in a burst of vibrant colour. "Oh, Mrs Cron! Can we buy some, please?"

"Of course. Why do you think I brought you along today? I need you to choose the prettiest ones for me."

Jane hurried to the flower seller, her red hair bouncing around her shoulders. She pored over each of the flowers, inhaling their scent and peering closely at their fragile petals. It made her think of her mother. She pressed a hand against the spot on her chest where she should have felt the locket. Jane felt a heavy pang of loss.

"What is the name of this flower?" she asked the stall owner. "And this one? This one?" She needed to know everything.

One day, she thought, she would surround herself with flowers just like these, and have herself the most beautiful flower shop in all of London.

When they arrived home, Daniel came running from the house to meet them. He grinned at the colourful array in Jane's arms. "Where did all these come from?"

"The flower seller was at the market today?" she told him. "I chose them myself. Do you like them?"

Daniel nodded, grinning.

"Come on, Jane," called Mrs Cron, "best get them in water."

Daniel trotted along beside them. "May I help?"

Jane frowned. "Your father won't like it. He doesn't like us playing together."

Daniel's face fell. "You heard that?"

Jane said nothing.

He pressed a gentle hand to her elbow. "My father's not home right now. I'll not tell him if you don't."

She managed a small smile.

Daniel nodded at the flowers, "So can I help?"

Jane grinned, thoughts of Mr Weir suddenly forgotten, "Of course."

The two children followed Mrs Cron into the kitchen and laid the flowers out across the table. Jane took three vases from the shelf and showed Daniel how to trim the stems.

"One day," she said, arranging the flowers neatly, "I'm going to have a flower shop all of my own. I'm going to sell the prettiest flowers in London."

She stopped suddenly. It was the first time she had ever dared voice the dream that had lived inside her for as long as she could remember. A part of her expected Daniel to scoff.

A flower shop? How will a girl from the workhouses ever own a flower shop?

But instead, he smiled, "I'll come and buy flowers from you every day."

CHAPTER 9

Two years in Mr Weir's household passed quickly.

JANE MISSED HER PARENTS DEARLY, and the first Christmas Day after her mother's death was terrible. She woke up in tears, clinging to Emily. She was fortunate in that it was a busy day. She and Mrs Cron had to prepare breakfast and then leave to dress in their best clothes to accompany the Weirs to church. It was traditional that the entire household attend Christmas service together on Christmas Day. On their return home, they quickly changed and set about preparing Christmas Dinner. Mr Weir had business associates over, so the meal was a grand affair. Jane would peel potatoes far quicker these days than in the workhouse, but she would burst into tears thinking about the glorious Christmas feasts that her mother prepared. She was sure that Mrs Cron noticed, but she said nothing and did not chastise her.

She would run errands for Mrs Cron. She would go to the market and purchase vegetables and visit the butcher to pick up the weekly meat order. As she walked the streets of London, she would stop at every pawnbroker she saw. She hoped that one day she would see her mother's precious locket in a window. She could not mistake it. The letters J and R engraved upon it. She would know it in an instant.

Of course, she had no idea how she might purchase it if she ever saw it. She had an idea she might mention it to Daniel. But that might be a step too far. The dilemma was never an issue for she never saw the locket.

. . .

As the months turned into years, she found truth in what Daniel had told her that very first day in the flower garden: that each day the loss began to hurt a little less. No longer did she want to cry herself to sleep each night. Her doll Emily was a beautiful reminder of the past, not a comfort on which she relied.

Mr Weir and Mrs Cron worked her hard and Jane was grateful. She liked to keep busy. But more than anything, she liked the times after her work was done when she and Daniel could escape into the garden or into the parlour to play together. They both knew their only chance to be together was when Mr Weir was not home, but the challenge of it only added to the excitement. When she was with Daniel, Jane's bitter memories of the workhouse had no power. When she was with Daniel, she did not think of how Mr Weir thought her unworthy. These were the times when, fleetingly, she was allowed to be a real child.

But one day, Daniel led her out into the garden, his face sombre. He sat on the grass beneath an enormous oak tree and tugged her down beside him. "Jane," he said huskily, "there's something I need to tell you."

Jane felt something tighten in her chest. She could tell by his tone that it was not good news. She looked up at him. Daniel had just turned eleven, but he looked suddenly tall and broad-shouldered like a grown man. When had such a thing happened?

"I'm being sent away," he said, eyes down. "I'm to stay with my uncle in Cambridge."

"No!" Jane cried. She bit her lip, embarrassed by her outburst. She swallowed heavily. "Is it because of me? Because your father doesn't like you spending time with me? Did he see us playing together?"

Daniel squeezed her elbow. "Oh, Jane, no. Of course not. I'm to go to school there. My father wants to make sure I'm ready for university in a few years." His voice was flat.

Jane said nothing. A part of her felt sure she was the reason he was being sent away, despite what Mr Weir had told his son.

"We'll still see each other," Daniel promised. "When I'm home for Christmas and summer holidays. We'll do all the things we used to do. Read and play in the garden and…"

Jane shook her head sadly. She knew things would never be the same again. "You won't want to see me," she said. "You'll go off to school in Cambridge and make real friends."

"Real friends?" Daniel repeated. "You *are* my real friend, Jane." He tried to catch her eye. "You're my best friend. You always will be."

She pushed away the tears that had escaped down her cheeks. "I'm just an orphan girl from the workhouse."

DANIEL LEFT TWO DAYS LATER. Jane watched from the window as the coach rolled away from the house, and then she ran down to her room and cried.

Once he had gone, the house felt empty. Working in the gardens just made her miss him more. Even visiting the flower market with Mrs Cron did little to raise her spirits. Seeing the flowers only made her think of Daniel and the way he had encouraged her when she had spoken of her flower shop. That dream would never happen.

It would be taken from her just like everything else.

True to his word, he returned to the house each summer and Christmas. Each time Jane saw him he looked more and more like a grown man. His shoulders were becoming wider, his legs longer, his voice deepening. Jane's feelings for him began to change into more than friendship.

Each time Daniel returned home, he would greet Jane with a warm embrace and that dimpled smile she had come to love. But what did he see in her, she wondered? A dirty, scrappy girl from the streets? Surely the day would soon come when he would arrive home from school and not want a thing to do with her.

On Jane's fourteenth Christmas, she felt sure this would be the year he would not want to see her. She decided she would not wait for him to cast her aside. When she heard his carriage approaching, she hurried into the kitchen and busied herself peeling a pile of vegetables.

She heard the front door open and heard footsteps in the hall and then footsteps on the stairs. Despite herself, she felt a fluttering in her chest.

She pushed it away and concentrated on the vegetables.

She could hear Mr Weir and Daniel chatting distantly. What were they talking about? His plans for university perhaps. A world in which Jane had no part. She moved her chopping board to the furthest corner of the kitchen so that she could not hear their voices. Hearing Daniel speak caused a tightening in her chest. The sound of his father's voice just filled Jane with dread.

In the past months, she had noticed Mr Weir's eyes beginning to linger on her young womanly body. He had started to ring for her more often. Each time he summoned her to his study, she felt a weight in her stomach that she was unable to shake. How was it possible, she wondered, that Daniel might be such a wonderful young man and his father so beastly?

When she had finished peeling the vegetables, Jane began to polish the windows, determined not to leave the kitchen. How long would Daniel be staying, she wondered. Days? Weeks? Could she manage not to cross his path for the duration of his presence? The thought filled her suddenly with sadness. Daniel was the dearest friend she had ever had. She hated the thought of him not being in her life. But they were from different worlds. Their lives were destined to go in opposite directions. The sooner she came to accept that, the better. Surely it was easiest for her to keep her distance. Try and ignore the way her heart raced whenever he came near.

A knock at the door made her start.

"Jane?"

At the sight of Daniel in the doorway, her breathing quickened. What was he doing in here? She knew Mr Weir would be furious if he caught his son in the kitchen chatting with the lowly workhouse runaway.

"Are you hiding from me?" he asked, a hint of hurt in his voice.

"Hiding? No. I—" she stopped, flustered. She turned back to the windows, polishing in earnest. She felt her ears burn.

Daniel's footsteps came towards her. "I've brought you a gift," he said.

Jane dared to turn and face him. Up close, she could see the gold flecks in his eyes. Her heart was racing. She swallowed heavily. "A gift?"

"Yes," Daniel smiled, revealing the dimple in his cheek. "It is Christmas, after all." From behind his back, he produced a rectangular package wrapped in deep red paper. He held it out towards her. "Open it."

Jane managed a small smile and peeled away the paper. Inside was a book with a blue and gold cover.

"Poetry of Robert Burns," Jane read.

"My uncle gave me a book of Robert Burns's work recently," Daniel told her. "It's beautiful. I wanted you to have a copy too. I know you'll enjoy it." He caught her eye. "Perhaps we might read it together? As we used to?"

Jane grinned. "I would like that very much," she said, her voice catching in her throat. She felt a sudden warmth in her chest.

Her thoughts of Daniel casting her aside suddenly seemed so foolish. She had a sudden urge to throw her arms around him. How she had missed him and how glad she was he had sought her out. How glad she had not hidden from him for his entire visit. She thought of sitting beside him by the hearth, reading the book of poetry he had chosen especially for her. She felt colour rising in her cheeks.

Daniel nodded towards the book. "There's something else. Open it."

Jane opened the cover curiously. She let out her

breath. Inside, a snowdrop had been pressed between the front pages. "It's beautiful," she whispered, caressing the fragile petals.

Daniel smiled. "I knew you'd like it. I found it on the roadside when I changed carriages on the way back from Cambridge," he said. "It made me think of you and the flower shop you will own one day."

Jane's cheeks flushed. Daniel remembered her dream of the flower shop. She didn't know whether to be flattered or embarrassed.

"Thank you," she said, her voice catching in her throat. "It's a wonderful present. I will treasure it always."

CHAPTER 10

Jane heard the bell ring from Mr Weir's study. "Miss Walker?" he bellowed.

Her stomach tightened. Damn the man. She knew he had been out late drinking the previous night and had hoped he might sleep the day away. Daniel was due to arrive home the following week and, despite herself, Jane had been unable to push away the excitement in her belly. But Mr Weir's bell was always able to dampen her spirits. Now seventeen, Jane found herself fighting off his advances on a regular basis.

She drew in her breath and strode up the stairs. She pushed open the door of Mr Weir's study. "Yes, sir? You rang for me?"

He grinned, showing a row of yellowing teeth. "Indeed I did." He rose from his desk chair and stumbled towards her. He stood close, his breath stale and smoky. She could smell old sweat and brandy on him. A half-drunk bottle sat open on the desk. She recoiled.

Mr Weir reached out and touched a strand of coppery hair that had fallen across Jane's eye. He lifted it from her cheek with a rough finger.

"Little Jane Walker," he drawled. "Who could have known that scrap from the streets would become such a fine example of womanhood?" He gave her a leering smile, making the muscles in her neck tighten. She tried to take a step backwards, but Mr Weir's hand shot out and snatched her arm. "Don't walk away from me, girl. We're speaking." He pulled her close. "A fine example of womanhood, indeed." His fingers worked their way up her arm.

Jane's stomach turned over. "Sir," she managed, "will you let go of me, please."

Mr Weir's grip tightened. Jane began to breathe hard and fast. She knew Mrs Cron was at the market. Mr Jacob, the gardener, had returned to his family for a holiday. She and Mr Weir were alone in the house.

He pulled her closer, his stale breath hot on her cheek. He lurched towards her, his lips seeking hers. Instinctively, Jane turned her head away.

"Don't you turn away from me," he hissed. "Have you forgotten everything I've done for you? Have you forgotten where you would be were it not for me?"

"No, sir," Jane coughed. "I've not forgotten."

"And don't you think you owe me a little? Don't you think you might repay my generosity?"

Jane swallowed hard. "I'm sorry, sir. I—"

Mr Weir yanked her towards him suddenly, dragging her towards the desk. Breathing hard, Jane tried to pull against him, but the man's large frame overpowered her, forcing her easily against the edge of the table.

"Help me!" she screamed, terror gripping her. "Someone! Please!"

They were alone in the house, yes, but perhaps someone might hear them from the street. Perhaps Mrs Cron might return home. Perhaps Mr Jacob might return unexpectedly. Perhaps, perhaps... She screamed again.

The door burst open. "Jane?" Daniel charged breathlessly into the study.

Mr Weir released his fistful of Jane's dress and

stumbled backwards. Jane fell to the floor, her legs giving way beneath her.

"Father!" Daniel's eyes were flashing. "What in blazes do you think you're doing? How dare you?"

Mr Weir tugged his jacket back over his shoulders. "What are you doing here, boy? You're not expected for another week."

"I thought to surprise you," Daniel said bitterly. "Although it seems you are the one with the surprises." He turned to Jane, offering her a hand up from the floor. "Are you all right?"

She nodded, straightening her skirts as she stood. "Yes. Thank you."

Daniel's fingers tightened around hers. He turned back to his father. "Don't you ever go near her again," he hissed. "Do you understand me?"

Taken aback by his son's outburst, Mr Weir said nothing. His wolfish eyes shifted from Daniel to Jane. She caught a faint, threatening smile in the corner of his mouth.

Daniel tugged her hand. "Let's leave." He gave his father a final glare before leading her out of the study and into the parlour.

Jane bent to stoke the fire. He took the poker from her trembling hand. "I can do that. Sit down.

You must be shaken." She heard a quiver of anger in his voice.

With the fire blazing, he sat beside her and pressed a warm hand to her cheek. "I'm sorry," he said. "I'm so sorry."

"You've no need to be sorry," said Jane. "You saved me."

"From my own father," he sighed angrily. "How long has this been going on?"

Jane looked at her hands, irrationally ashamed. "He tries such a thing from time to time. Usually when he's been drinking."

"Has he ever…?"

She shook her head. "I've always managed to get away. But today, he was… different. Angrier. He'd been drinking excessively, I suppose." She stared at her clasped hands. "I don't know what I would have done if you hadn't arrived when you did. If you hadn't been there for me…"

Daniel slid his arm around her shoulder and pulled her close. Jane's fear began to dissolve in the gentleness of his touch.

"I'll always be here for you, Jane," he said softly. "Always." He kissed the top of her head.

She closed her eyes. She tried to let Daniel's closeness and the heat of the fire sear away the last of her nerves. Though she felt better, her heart was unable to slow.

I will always be here for you.

She knew of course that Daniel meant what he had said. And as long as they were in the same house, she was safe from the master. But soon Daniel would return to Cambridge. Mrs Cron would go to the markets each day. And she and the lecherous drunk would be alone in the house once again.

CHAPTER 11

Daniel's week-long visit flew by. After the incident, Mr Weir had avoided both his son and Jane, leaving them free to spend time together. Each day, Jane rushed through her chores, desperate to disappear into the parlour or the snowy garden with Daniel. She was sure Mrs Cron had noticed her sloppy workmanship but the old woman had been kind enough not to mention it.

The morning before Daniel was due to return to Cambridge, Jane made her way up to the master's study with his coffee pot, as she did each morning. Since the incident, he had said nothing to her, avoiding her eyes each morning as she set the pot on his desk and poured him a cup.

Was he angry with her? Or just ashamed of his behaviour? She couldn't tell. But fear of what he might do once Daniel left sat in the pit of her stomach.

She tapped lightly on the door. "Mr Weir? I've brought your coffee."

There was no answer.

She tried again. "Sir?" When he didn't respond, Jane pushed the door open and tiptoed into the study. She gasped. Mr Weir was slumped motionless in his desk chair, his head drooped forward.

Heart pounding, Jane set the coffee pot on the desk and reached gingerly for his arm. His body was cold and stiff. She stumbled backwards in shock, knocking the coffee pot and spilling its contents across the desk. She raced from the room, calling for Daniel. He burst out of his bedroom and grabbed her shoulders.

"What is it, Jane? What's happened?"

"Your father," she said breathlessly. "I think he's…" she swallowed hard. "I think he's dead."

Something unreadable passed across Daniel's face. His eyes became suddenly devoid of emotion. "Where is he?" he asked stiffly.

"Upstairs." Jane led him into the study, tensing again at the sight of the body in the chair. She hovered in the doorway as Daniel approached his father. He pressed two fingers to the man's neck.

"You were right," he said, his voice strangely hollow. "We ought to fetch the doctor. Try and determine the cause of death."

JANE ESCAPED to the kitchen when the doctor arrived. Her heart was still racing. She could not shake the feel of Mr Weir's cold body beneath her fingers.

"Too much drink," Mrs Cron said loudly. "Mark my words, girl, that'll be what's killed him. Too much drink."

Jane said nothing. In spite of herself, she couldn't silence the flicker of joy dancing inside her. With Mr Weir gone, she would be safe. She kept her eyes downcast, terrified her face would betray her inappropriate feelings.

Mrs Cron peered through the window. "The doctor is leaving," she reported. "No doubt the undertakers will be here soon for the body."

Jane joined her at the window and peered through the glass. Daniel was standing alone outside the front door. He looked suddenly young and alone.

Mrs Cron nudged her, "Go to him."

Jane hesitated, "I don't know... He's just lost his father."

"That's exactly why you ought to go to him. You're the only person who has brought him comfort since his mother died. He ought not to be alone right now. And I'm sure you're the only person he'll be willing to see."

JANE LEFT the house through the servant's entrance and walked towards the front door. "Daniel?"

He turned, giving her a faint smile.

"Won't you come inside? It's so cold out here."

He nodded and they made their way into the parlour together. They sat by side on the couch. It had been barely a week since they had sat here in such a way, their shoulders pressed together, Daniel comforting Jane over Mr Weir's attack. Now she was the one taking his hand, the one mumbling words of soft condolence.

"I'm so sorry," she told him.

Daniel squeezed her hand. "The doctor suspects he died of a heart attack. Too much work and too much drink." He stared down at their intertwined fingers. He opened his mouth to speak, then stopped.

Jane frowned, "What is it? You can tell me. You can tell me anything."

Daniel drew in his breath, "I know it's terrible, but there's a part of me that is not sorry he's gone. I know he never treated you right. And I'm not sure I'll ever forgive him for what he did to you last week."

"Your father had some good in him," Jane said huskily. "Your father bought me from the workhouse. He gave me a home. A job. Despite anything else he may have done, I've not forgotten that."

Daniel's pale smile returned. "I'm so glad he did. I don't know what I would do if I didn't have you in my life."

Jane felt desire and emotion swirl inside her. She slid her arms around Daniel's shoulders, holding him tightly as his tears left damp circles on her shoulder.

CHAPTER 12

It was several months before Jane saw Daniel again. In his absence, she and Mrs Cron kept the house clean and polished, awaiting the return of the new master of the house.

Two days before Christmas his carriage again rolled through the gates. Jane's heart began to speed. She began to chop her vegetables at double speed.

Mrs Cron chuckled, "Something got you excited, my girl?"

Jane's cheeks flushed. She wiped her hands on her apron. "I'm going to meet him," she said boldly. Now Mr Weir was gone, there was no one to stop her and Daniel from being together. Her heart fluttered at the thought.

But as she made her way upstairs, she heard a second pair of footsteps entering the house and heard another man's voice speaking with Daniel. She caught sight of a tall, grey-haired man with a striking resemblance to Mr Weir. She swallowed heavily and tried to slip back into the kitchen.

"Jane!" Daniel cried excitedly. His face lit up at the sight of her. She couldn't help returning his smile. He hurried towards her and planted a gentle kiss on her cheek. "It's so wonderful to see you," he gushed, taking one of her hands in both of his and squeezing.

He gestured to the tall man, "Jane, this is my uncle. Father's brother. He has been kind enough to come home for Christmas with me this year. Uncle, this is Jane Walker. A very dear friend of mine."

The man glanced at Jane's food-stained apron but managed a small smile. "Miss Walker," he said, nodding his head in greeting.

She bobbed a polite curtsey.

Daniel squeezed her hand again. "I've so much to tell you, Jane. So many stories about Cambridge. I—"

"Can we be expecting supper soon, Miss Walker?" Daniel's uncle interrupted. "My nephew and I have travelled a long way. And I'd like some tea, if you please."

Jane turned from Daniel and straightened her shoulders. "Of course, sir. Supper will not be long. I'll fetch the tea for you right away."

"I'M SORRY ABOUT MY UNCLE," Daniel apologised the next day, appearing at the door of the kitchen. "He doesn't mean any offence."

Jane put down her cloth and gave him a small smile. "I know. He was just reminding me of my place. He was right to do so."

A look of regret passed across Daniel's face, but he said nothing. "Will you walk with me?" he asked after a moment. "The snowdrops are blooming early again."

Jane smiled, then nodded at the pot she was scrubbing, "I've work to do."

Daniel gave her a playful smile, "I'm the master of the house now, Jane. And if I wish you to take a walk with me instead of washing the dishes, then I think you ought to do so."

. . .

"You said you had much to tell me." She walked close to Daniel as they made their way out into the garden. The frosty grass crunched beneath their feet. The pale sunlight made everything glitter.

Daniel gave a short chuckle, "Nothing of any importance. Just stories from Cambridge. I've been so looking forward to seeing you. I wanted to tell you everything that has happened since we last saw each other." He glanced at her shyly. "But I'm sure my tales of foolish boys' pranks are of little interest to you."

Jane reached for his arm, "Of course they are!" She wanted to hear everything. Wanted to know how Daniel filled his days. Who did he spend his time with? Where did they go? What did they do?

She listened intently as he told her of his long country walks and boating on the river. He told her of his friends, his tutors, and the old woman who cleaned the halls and claimed she could see ghosts. It warmed Jane's heart to have him share so much with her.

She smiled, "You sound happy. I'm so glad of it. After your father…"

Daniel stared at his feet as he walked. "My father and I…" he said after a moment, "we were never close. Of course, I would never have wished any ill luck on him. But..." he exhaled sharply, searching for the right words. "I'll never forget what he did to you, Jane. I'll never forget the wildness in his eyes when I found you in the study that night. I'm not sure I'll ever truly be able to forgive him." His hand slid down her arm and their fingers interlaced.

Jane's heart leapt into her chest.

"I'm glad to know he can no longer hurt you," Daniel said. "I don't think I would have been able to go back to Cambridge if I had had to leave you alone with him."

Jane turned to him in surprise. "You would have stayed here for me?"

"Of course," he squeezed her hand. "After the... incident... before my father died, I was making plans to stay in London. I couldn't bear the thought of leaving you alone with him."

Jane let out her breath. "I had no idea."

"I told you I would always be here for you," said Daniel, meeting her eyes. "I meant it." He stopped walking. "Look." They had reached the garden bed the two of them had replanted together when they were children. "Snowdrops."

Jane smiled. A fine layer of frost lay across the garden, the white flowers glinting with ice. Jane reached out and touched one, hearing a faint tinkling as the wind rustled the frozen leaves. "They're beautiful."

She dared to glance at Daniel. Was he thinking of the pressed snowdrop he had given her? The pressed snowdrop that still sat on her nightstand.

Their eyes met. Daniel reached out and pushed a stray strand of hair beneath Jane's cap. He leaned in and kissed her gently. Warmth flooded her body. Too soon, he pulled away.

"I'd do anything for you, Jane," he said softly, his lips close to hers. "You know that, don't you?"

She brushed her gloved hand across his cheek. "And I would do anything for you."

CHAPTER 13

For the rest of the day, Jane was unable to wipe away the enormous smile that had spread across her face. Her whole body was alight, her heart refusing to slow. Was this what it felt like to be in love?

She could feel Mrs Cron's eyes on her as they prepared supper. "What's got you in such a state, child?" the old woman asked with a smile.

Jane felt her cheeks turn crimson. "Nothing."

Mrs Cron laughed to herself, her eyes dark and knowing. When she was sure the housekeeper wasn't looking, Jane reached up and pressed her fingers to her mouth, feeling the place where Daniel's lips had touched hers.

But that evening as she was clearing the supper table, Jane heard voices coming from the parlour. Although she couldn't make out their words, she could tell Daniel and his uncle were in a heated conversation.

Jane put down the dishes and pressed her ear to the door.

"You can't be seen with that girl," Daniel's uncle barked.

Daniel sighed loudly, "Of course I can. She's my friend. My *best* friend."

A snort. "She's more than a friend, judging by what I saw you two doing in the garden. Do I need to remind you of the importance of finding a good wife? Ensuring you will find someone to provide you with an heir of good standing? I'm sure any potential brides would not be happy to hear you've been gallivanting about the gardens with the pot maid!"

The bitterness in the man's voice made the back of Jane's neck prickle with hatred.

"You sound just like my father," Daniel said coldly.

"Good. My brother was a wise and successful man. He has built an empire stretching the length of this country. It's time you began to think like him also. You are a very eligible bachelor now, Daniel. You could secure any wife you wished. Things with that girl need to end now." His voice was firm.

Jane felt her throat tighten. She waited for Daniel to argue on her behalf but there was only silence. Tears pricked her eyes as she snatched up the supper dishes and hurried back to the kitchen.

DANIEL WAS WAITING for her the next morning when she entered the parlour to light the fire. He was perched on the edge of an armchair, his eyes underlined with shadow.

"You've not slept," said Jane.

"Barely," he admitted. He stared intently into his hands. "Jane, can we speak?" His voice was husky and strained. Jane felt something turn over in her stomach.

No, she wanted to say. *No, we cannot speak.* She knew anything to come from his mouth in such a state would not be good. But she nodded wordlessly. Daniel gestured to the armchair opposite his, but she shook her head, hovering beside the hearth and clasping her hands across her chest. Daniel stood so his eyes were level with hers. He dared to look up at her.

"What happened in the garden yesterday..." he began, "it was a mistake."

Jane said nothing. Daniel's words hung in the air. Despite the obvious regret in his voice, his statement felt cruel and cold.

"I'm sorry," he continued. "Truly. I shouldn't have done it. I just..." He sighed again and rubbed his eyes. "I was so happy to see you, I didn't think. I acted rashly. But..."

"Your uncle has been speaking to you," Jane cut in, her voice caught in her throat.

"You heard that conversation?"

She said nothing. Tears began to well behind her eyes. She stared at her feet, willing herself not to cry.

A mistake.

Nothing had made her feel as happy or as alive as Daniel's kiss. A kiss that had made her sure that she was in love with him. And here he was calling it a mistake. Anger began to bubble beneath her skin.

When he didn't speak again, Jane said bitterly,

THE CHRISTMAS ORPHAN

"Yesterday you told me you would do anything for me. And now you will not even stand up to your uncle to defend me."

Daniel gave a faint accepting nod. "I ought to have, I know. But…" He wrung his hands together as though trying to search for the right words. "The thing is, Jane, I know my uncle is right. I have to marry someone of… someone who…"

"Someone who didn't come from the workhouse?" Jane finished coldly.

"Someone with connections," Daniel said. His carefully chosen words did nothing to ease the ache in Jane's chest. The tears she had been fighting slipped suddenly down her cheeks. She swiped at them angrily. At the sight of her tears, Daniel stepped close and pressed an impulsive hand to her cheek.

"I wish things were different," he said. "Truly. And I'm more sorry than you will ever know. I never wanted to hurt you."

Jane longed to pull away, but the feel of Daniel's palm against her skin kept her frozen. He planted a soft kiss on her cheek. "I will always love you, Jane," he said, his words bringing a fresh flood of tears.

It was to be expected, she told herself. After all, look at her, standing here in her housemaid's uniform, ready to light the fires. She had always known that she was not worthy of Daniel. Always knew the fragility of what existed between them would one day be torn away.

CHAPTER 14

Ten years had passed since Mr Weir's death. Ten long years since Jane and Daniel had consoled each other in the parlour, their fingers intertwined. Ten years since the kiss in the garden. And ten years since Daniel's uncle had convinced him to break off their relationship.

Jane's love for him had not faded. She longed for such a thing to happen. Longed to wake and find the painful feelings gone.

Ten years had passed, but still Jane laid the fires and blacked the hearths for Daniel's household. She still peeled vegetables and scrubbed pots for Mrs Cron and kept her eyes averted from guests like the workhouse girl she was.

She still visited the markets and the butchers.

But these days she rarely stopped to stare into the windows of pawnbrokers. She knew her mother's locket was lost forever.

But now the household consisted of Daniel's wife, Naomi, and their one-year-old son, Nathaniel.

Naomi and Daniel had married two years earlier in a lavish ceremony at St Mary's. Daniel had begged Jane to attend.

"You're my dearest friend," he told her. "I just couldn't get married without you there."

"I'm sorry," Jane had told him. "I couldn't. It would not be right, and you know it." It would not be right, she had said, for a housemaid to sit among guests from the upper classes of society. And she had clung to that excuse, while underneath it knowing the truth: she couldn't bear to watch the man she had loved since childhood marry another woman. She had been angry at Daniel for insisting. Surely he knew how she felt.

When Daniel had first brought his new wife home, the dislike between the two women had been instantaneous. Daniel had introduced Jane as a friend rather than a servant. Naomi had been quick to remind her of her place.

Once her husband had left the room, she

followed Jane into the kitchen. "Listen to me, Miss Walker," she said, her voice clipped and icy. "It is clear to me that you and my husband have a past. One I do not wish to know about." Her cheeks were pink with anger. "But from now on, I expect you to know your place. And that place is down here with a scrubbing brush in your hand. Not gallivanting about the house with my husband."

Jane clenched her teeth, determined not to let her anger show. She looked Naomi up and down. Her blonde hair was piled on top of her head, her cheeks rouged, lips pinched. She reminded Jane of a doll she had owned in the long-ago days before her father had died.

Daniel had told her his wife-to-be was the daughter of a great shipping magnate. Jane had pretended to be interested. Pretended to be pleased he would marry into a fine, upstanding family. Did Daniel love her, Jane found herself wondering as she stood looking into the bitter face of the new Mrs Weir? Or had he simply obeyed his uncle's wishes by marrying a woman of good standing?

"Do you understand me, Miss Walker?"

Jane met Naomi's stern gaze. "Of course."

Naomi narrowed her eyes, "Of course, *Mrs Weir.*"

Jane tightened her jaw, her heart pounding with anger. "Of course, Mrs Weir."

When Naomi left, Jane flung a chopping board across the room in a wild fit of rage.

"Goodness me." She turned at the sound of Mrs Cron's voice. Colour rose in Jane's cheeks, ashamed to have been caught mid-outburst. But Mrs Cron just wrapped her arms around her, the way she had when Jane was a child.

"I know it's difficult," she said gently, pulling Jane into her.

Tears pricked her eyes. She hurriedly blinked them away. She had known for many years that she had no future with Daniel. But deep down, she had always harboured a tiny flicker of hope that things might change. But the presence of Daniel's new wife had crushed that last tiny spark of optimism.

Daniel and Naomi's son was born a year after the wedding. On the day of his birth, Daniel had knocked on Jane's bedroom door with the baby in his arms. Emily still sat on her bed during the day and snuggled up inside with her at night. She knew it was stupid and childish, but it gave her comfort.

"I want you to meet my son," he told her, his eyes glowing with love and pride. "Nathaniel."

Jane peered down at the tiny bundle asleep in his father's arms. Her chest ached. How she wished she had been the one to give Daniel a son. She forced herself to be happy for him. She touched the baby's smooth forehead, then kissed Daniel on the cheek.

"Congratulations," she managed. "He is beautiful."

Daniel's smile widened. "Thank you." He looked about him. He had not been inside Jane's bedroom since they were children. Even then, it had only ever been for fleeting moments, aware, even at nine years old of the inappropriateness of it.

He looked back at her. "I've missed you, Jane."

She didn't answer. She had missed him too, desperately, though she saw him every day. Saw him as the master, the head of the household, to whom she had to curtsey and obey. She missed Daniel, her friend.

"And the Mistress?" Jane asked, feeling

suddenly uncomfortable at the closeness of Daniel and the baby. "She is well?"

He looked slightly surprised at her question. "Yes," he said throatily. "She is well." He cleared his throat. "I'd best get back to her."

Jane nodded, "Yes, you'd best do that."

She closed the door after him and listened to his footsteps disappear.

CHAPTER 15

Jane was cleaning the windows in the parlour when a movement in the garden caught her eye. She could see the mistress by the flower bed, gesturing wildly to Mr Jacob, the gardener. Naomi was pointing forcefully to the rows of green shoots Jane had recently planted while the old man nodded morosely. Then Mr Jacob shuffled off to the tool shed and returned with a shovel in his hands. He began to dig at the garden, upturning the earth where Jane had so lovingly planted the seeds.

Jane threw down her polishing rag and raced into the garden. At the sight of her, Mr Jacob stopped digging.

"What are you doing?" she cried.

The gardener hung his head. "I'm sorry, Miss Walker, Mrs Weir, she—"

"I've told Mr Jacob I want these flowers taken out," Naomi cut in.

Jane could feel her cheeks flushing with rage. "Taken out?" she repeated. "Why?"

"That's none of your business."

Jane clenched her fists. Had Daniel told Naomi about the way he and Jane had planted the garden when they were children? Was she doing this out of spite? Jane felt suddenly sure of it.

"Please put the shovel down," Jane told Mr Jacob with as much composure as she could muster.

Naomi's eyes flashed. "I give the orders around here, Miss Walker."

"What is all this?" They turned to see Daniel striding across the lawn.

"She wants to destroy the garden," Jane told him breathlessly.

"Destroy the garden?" he looked at Naomi expectantly.

She huffed, "I do not want to destroy the garden. I simply want to use it for something else. I thought to plant a few herbs."

"There is plenty of space in the rest of the garden," Daniel told her. "Choose another plot. This was my mother's flower garden. It has been Jane's flower garden since the very day she arrived here. She brought it back to life. And so it will stay."

Jane wanted to throw her arms around him. Naomi's cheeks coloured with rage. She turned abruptly and marched back into the house.

THAT NIGHT, as Jane made her way past the parlour, she could hear mumbled words between the couple. It had been here, ten years ago, Jane thought, that she had stood listening to Daniel's uncle talk him out of his relationship with Jane. Ten years since she had stood at the door and heard him proclaim her unworthy.

Ten years since Daniel had meekly agreed and come to find her in the kitchen.

But as their voices rose, Jane could hear Daniel leaping to her defence. "There was no reason for you to destroy that garden. Jane had every right to be upset."

"This isn't about the garden," Naomi hissed. "It's about you embarrassing me in front of the staff. Taking the side of that pot maid instead of your own wife."

Jane burned with anger. She pressed her ear against the door.

"You were being unreasonable," said Daniel. "That's why I took Jane's side."

"You care for her," Naomi said bitterly.

"Of course I care for her. We've been friends since childhood."

"No, Daniel, you care for her as more than a friend. I see the way you look at her."

Jane felt a sudden quickening of her heart, but Daniel said hurriedly: "That's ridiculous."

"Ridiculous?" Naomi spat. "Do you think me a fool?"

For a few moments, no one spoke. Then Jane heard Daniel say, "The garden stays."

Things between Naomi and Daniel remained tense. Jane could sense the coldness between them as they sat through wordless suppers and mumbled terse goodnights from opposite ends of the parlour. Jane could see strain behind Daniel's eyes. She longed to console him, comfort him, but knew of course that she could never do so. She was clearly the cause of the conflict, after all. Not to mention a lowly housemaid scooped from the workhouse.

MEALTIMES WERE UNCOMFORTABLE. Daniel and Naomi rarely said a word to each other, while Jane and Mrs Cron shuffled around them, trying to pretend they were invisible.

But Jane did not feel invisible. She could feel Naomi's dagger eyes on her whenever she entered the room. Edgy from the tension, Jane reached across the table for the empty plates, knocking the gravy jug over onto the table.

Naomi's voice sparked suddenly. "I want this girl gone," she snapped, glaring at her husband. "I've had enough."

Daniel looked aghast at her sudden outburst. "Don't be foolish," he hissed, trying to keep his voice low.

"Foolish?" Naomi hissed. "How dare you suggest I'm being foolish? You are clearly in love with your kitchen maid."

At the sudden accusation, Jane's heart began to race. Mrs Cron lowered her head and shuffled from the room. Jane gripped the gravy jug, unsure what to do. Surely she couldn't stay here and witness this, nor could she leave the dining room with her duties unfulfilled. She felt Naomi's eyes bore into her.

"Yes," she said coldly as though sensing Jane's dilemma, "you ought to leave, too. Leave the house. Leave our lives."

Daniel's hand shot out, clutching Jane's elbow. "She's not going anywhere," he told Naomi firmly. "I make the decisions as to who our staff will be, and Jane will never be fired. She will always have a home here. I'm sorry if you don't like it, but that's just the way things are."

Naomi's eyes flashed. She opened her mouth to speak but said nothing.

Daniel looked up at Jane. "Finish clearing the table," he told her gently. "I'm sorry you had to hear all this." Their eyes met and, for a moment they were teenagers again, standing together in the snowy garden.

Daniel pulled his eyes from hers and looked across the table at Naomi. She stared bitterly at his fingers, still clutching Jane's elbow. He let his hand fall. Jane scooped the dishes from the table and hurried from the room.

CHAPTER 16

A bell rang suddenly, calling Jane to Daniel's study. She sucked in her breath and put down the scrubbing brush. She and Daniel had not spoken since Naomi's outburst at the dinner table three days before.

Could she trust him to keep his word and not fire her? How desperately she wanted to believe him, but she knew Daniel had crumbled under pressure before. For all his speaking of his affection for her, she knew the gaping social divide between them would never go away. Nor, it seemed, would his wife's passionate dislike for her.

Her heart was racing by the time she reached his study. She knocked nervously.

"Jane," Daniel smiled when he saw her. He

stood from behind his desk. "Please come in. Sit down."

In the study with him was an older man with greying hair and a long, straight nose. He wore a black frock coat and grey cravat. Jane entered hesitantly and perched on the edge of the chair. The man in the coat extended his hand.

"Miss Walker. My name is Albert Doran. I'm a solicitor with Davidson, Wells and Doran. A partner in the firm."

Jane shook his hand cautiously. "A solicitor?" Her heart began to race. Was she in trouble? Had Naomi engineered this?

The man smiled, soothing her unease a little. "I'm pleased to tell you I have good news. You, Miss Walker, are the sole beneficiary of a benefactor whose name I am unable to reveal as yet. But I can tell you that you will be receiving an immediate cash gift of three hundred pounds, along with a monthly allowance of eleven pounds, 3 shillings."

Jane stared in disbelief, "What? A benefactor?"

Mr Doran smiled, "I'm sure this comes as quite a shock."

"A shock," Jane managed. "Yes, of course it's a

shock. You can't tell me anything about who has given me such a sum?"

"I'm afraid not," said the solicitor. "The benefactor has requested he remains anonymous at this point."

Jane's thoughts knocked together. It had to be Daniel, of course. He had the funds. His business empire seemed to grow by the month.

She dared to glance at him. He had a broad smile across his face.

"Isn't this amazing news, Jane? Now you will be able to purchase your flower shop. Just like you've always wanted."

"The flower shop. Yes." Her heart pounded against her ribs. Nothing felt real. With this money, of course, she would no longer be a housemaid to Daniel and Naomi. It was clever of Daniel, for certain. Jane would be taken care of, and Naomi would be pleased to have her gone. It was an elegant solution to the problem.

She turned away from him, unsure whether to be insanely grateful or wild with anger. She straightened her shoulders. If Daniel wanted to pay her way and gift her with the business she had always dreamed of, she would certainly take it.

She sucked in her breath, imbued with a

sudden determination. It was time to move on and truly make something of her life.

Daniel had Naomi. It was time to leave her childish infatuation with him in the past. Such a thing would hurt, for certain; but it could be no more painful than seeing the man she loved parading around the house with his wife and son each day.

Lilies, she thought. *Bluebells, roses. The finest flower shop in all of London.* She said it to herself again, to strengthen her resolve.

Lilies, bluebells, roses. The finest flower shop in all of London.

She looked Mr Doran in the eye. "Thank you for bringing this news. It is indeed wonderful to hear."

CHAPTER 17

Jane found a small shop on a street corner near Islington, close to where she had lived with her family before her father had died. Above the shop was a small but beautifully decorated set of rooms. The rooms were filled constantly with a welcoming and fresh floral scent. Just being in the area in which she had been born brought Jane a great sense of peace. Seeing her much-dreamed-of business come to life was nothing short of thrilling.

Emily came with her and remained on her bed during the day and in her bed at night. Now she was closer to the area she truly called home, Emily became even more important. When she slept, she would still see her father's warm eyes dancing in front of the fire that Christmas.

Roses, she called her flower shop, a fitting tribute to her mother.

The business grew steadily in its first year, the word spreading quickly about Jane's knowledge and passion for her work. She hired a young girl and boy from the workhouse in Whitechapel to serve as her apprentices. Flowers, she thought, had brightened those grey days of her childhood. Perhaps she might do the same for these children. She treated them well.

Jane had felt a great rush of relief when she had left the Weirs' house; a place in which she had lived and worked for the past twenty years. There had been many happy times in the place, of course, but plenty of heartbreak too.

She had thrown her arms around Mrs Cron and squeezed her tightly. The old woman had been like a mother to her, and Jane knew she would miss her desperately.

Mrs Cron pushed aside her tears, "I'm so proud of you, my girl. And so happy for you." She gave Jane's hands a tight squeeze. "I'll be coming to buy all my flowers from you now, so make sure you put the best ones aside for me."

Jane's farewell to Daniel had been formal and business-like. A shake of the hand. Thanks for all his support over the years. She had felt him trying to look behind her eyes, trying to catch hold of a little of the closeness they had shared. But she had been determined. She would leave her love for Daniel in the past where it belonged. He gave her fingers a slight squeeze as she made to pull her hand from his.

"Good luck, Jane," his voice was throaty. "I'll miss you."

Determined not to cry, Jane nodded and then turned to leave the room.

She stopped and turned and finally managed to speak. "Thank you for everything you have done."

She walked from the house out into the street and befitting of her new status in life, hailed a cab to Islington. As the horses drew away, the clip-clopping of their hooves on the cobbles reminded her of the footsteps of the matron along the corridors of the workhouse. She felt an overwhelming sense of sadness and, as the streets of London passed by, the tears flowed down her cheeks.

. . .

But despite her best intentions, Daniel was still a part of her life. He would come into the shop regularly with that handsome, boyish grin on his face, his eyes lighting up when he saw her. Each time, Jane's heart would leap in her chest. Curse him, she would think to herself. Curse her wayward feelings. As much as she loved him, she wished he would disappear from her life. They would never be together. How could she move on when he continued to pay her visits in this way?

Each time he walked into the shop, he would kiss her cheek and ask about the business, lavishing her with compliments about how beautiful the shop was. And each time, Jane would be tormented by her conflicting emotions: rage at his getting rid of her and gratitude at his generosity that had allowed her to live out her dream. She wished she could ask him to buy his flowers elsewhere but knew such a thing was not possible. Not when he was the one who had made the shop a reality.

They would make stilted small talk and Daniel would leave with an armful of flowers for his wife. Jane would watch him leave, exhaling with relief that she might be spared the heartache of his visits for another few weeks.

. . .

Late one afternoon, Jane was about to lock up the shop when she saw a familiar figure approach. Mrs Cron trudged towards her, pulling a large handkerchief from her pocket and mopping her brow that glistened in the August heat.

"Mrs Cron," Jane gave her a wide smile but the old woman's face was morose. Jane felt something turn over in her stomach. "Has something happened?"

Mrs Cron took Jane's hand in both of hers and pressed it to her breast. "It's good to see you, little one. It's been months. And would you look at this place? I'd heard you were doing well. I'm so happy to see it." Her voice was flat.

"Has something happened?" Jane asked again.

Mrs Cron looked at her feet, "I'm afraid I have some bad news. It's the mistress. She... she's gone. Passed away giving birth. The child, too, I'm sorry to say." The old woman pushed away a stray tear.

Jane's stomach somersaulted. She squeezed Mrs Cron's hand, "That's dreadful. Poor Daniel. He must be inconsolable."

She nodded, "He's in a state, of course. He's got little Nathaniel to care for. Keeps telling me he doesn't know how the boy will manage without a mother."

Jane swallowed heavily. "Nathaniel has a wonderful father. I know he will manage just fine."

Mrs Cron gave a faint smile. "It was Daniel who asked me to come here," she told Jane. "He has requested that you supply the flowers for the funeral."

"Of course. Tell him I will take care of everything. It's the least I can do."

JANE STAYED up late the next night preparing a beautiful floral tribute for the funeral. She carefully arranged the deep red roses, inhaling their luxurious scent.

She couldn't bring herself to feel anything for Naomi, but she was determined to give her and the baby a beautiful funeral, for Daniel's sake.

How she longed to see him; how she longed to comfort him, to sit beside him on the couch in the parlour and squeeze his hand in hers, telling him everything would be all right. But of course, the time for such things had passed. She was sure Daniel would be mourning the loss of his wife and child far more deeply than he had mourned his father.

But despite her emotions, Jane couldn't help but think of how it had felt when their hands were intertwined. She couldn't help but think of the way her heart had leapt into her chest when their lips touched in the garden. She hurriedly pushed the thoughts away and returned to arranging the roses.

CHAPTER 18

Daniel's visits to the flower shop ceased. Of course, Jane thought sadly. He had no one to buy flowers for anymore. This was what she had wanted, she reminded herself, for Daniel to no longer be a part of her life. But she thought of him often, wondering how he was coping, wishing to comfort him. On more than one occasion, she even considered paying a visit to the house to see how he and Nathaniel were faring. Each time, she had decided against it. It was best this way, she told herself. Best for them to become no more to each other than memories. Perhaps with Daniel out of her life, she might even find someone to love.

. . .

CHRISTMAS WAS FAST APPROACHING. The shop was filled with mistletoe and holly, reminding Jane of the winter her father had taught her how to cut holly from the bush in the park. It reminded her of how she used to sell sprigs of it in the square before she and her mother were forced into the workhouse. How vivid her memories were of that time. She could still remember standing in the square with her flowers clutched to her chest while snow fluttered down around her. She could still remember the disappointment she had felt when she had been forced to trudge back to Whitechapel with empty pockets. She could still remember the horror when she had arrived home to find the tenement room emptied.

Each Christmas since she began working for the Weirs, Jane had given Mrs Cron a small gift as a thank-you for scooping her from the streets that day. A thank you for helping her build a life. Mrs Cron had been the closest to a mother to Jane since Rose's death. She couldn't begin to imagine where she might be without her. She would continue the tradition of the gift this year, Jane thought, even if it meant venturing back to the house full of so many memories.

. . .

THE CHRISTMAS ORPHAN

It was Christmas Eve. She could not put off her visit any longer. Sucking in her courage, Jane made her way out into the snow and hailed a cab, the gift for Mrs Cron clutched to her chest. She would go in through the servants' entrance and hurry into the kitchen to see the housekeeper without any need to lay eyes on Daniel.

As the carriage clattered through the crowded streets, Jane was hit with a wave of guilt. She had not seen Daniel since Naomi and the baby had died. She had not sought him out to offer her condolences. She had put her own feelings ahead of his. The shame sat heavy in her stomach.

When she arrived at the house, she let herself hurriedly into the kitchen. A fire was blazing in the hearth, making her cold cheeks burn.

Mrs Cron's lined face lit up as she pulled Jane into her arms. "Oh, Jane, it's been too long, my girl. It's so lovely to see you."

Jane took off her gloves and handed the old lady the wrapped gift. "This is for you. Merry Christmas."

Mrs Cron beamed. "Oh, Jane, you shouldn't have."

She managed a laugh, "You say that every year."

The old woman smiled. "Indeed I do. And every year I mean it."

Jane walked around the kitchen that had once been so familiar to her. She remembered standing at the counter learning to knead bread dough with Mrs Cron on the day after she had arrived at the Weirs. It felt like a lifetime ago.

"How is everything here?" she asked, her voice trapped in her throat. "How are Daniel and Nathaniel?"

"They are doing well," said Mrs Cron. "The first few months were difficult, of course, but things are getting easier for them every day. You were right when you said the boy had a wonderful father."

Jane smiled.

"Will you stay for a little tea?"

She shook her head. "I'd best be getting back." Best she disappear before she crossed paths with Daniel. "My apprentices are alone in the shop and the weather is…" Jane faded out as a figure appeared in the doorway.

"Jane," Daniel said stiffly. "I thought I heard your voice."

She opened her mouth to speak, but nothing came out.

"What are you doing here?" he asked.

"I have a Christmas present for Mrs Cron." She turned to look at the housekeeper, but she had vanished suddenly, leaving the two of them alone in the kitchen.

Swallowing heavily, she turned back to face Daniel. He was as handsome as ever. How she had missed him. Jane had a sudden urge to throw herself into his arms. Instead she said, "Forgive me. I ought to have come to see you after Naomi…"

"And I ought to have come to thank you for the beautiful flowers you arranged for the funeral."

Jane gave a small smile, "Perhaps we might forgive one another?"

Daniel nodded towards the garden. His lips turned up, making the dimple in his cheek appear. "Only if you will walk with me."

THE SNOW HAD EASED as Jane and Daniel stepped out into the garden. A fine layer of white glittered across the grounds. Their boots crunched softly as they walked. Despite herself, Jane's memory flickered back to that day in the garden ten years ago. The day Daniel had kissed her and told her he would do anything for her.

She dared a sideways glance at him. His hands

were dug into his pockets, his eyes on his feet. He looked up suddenly, their eyes meeting. And the years fell away. They were children again, playing in the garden, speaking of hideouts and fox holes. Impulsively, Jane took his arm. She was relieved when he didn't pull away.

"I'm so sorry about Naomi and the baby," she told him. "Truly."

Walking beside Daniel, she thought of the pain he must have gone through, burying his wife and child. She meant every word, she realised. True, she had never liked Naomi, but she would not have wished such a terrible fate upon her. She would certainly never have wished such a terrible fate on Daniel and his son.

"Thank you," Daniel murmured. He kept his eyes downcast. "It was a boy," he told her. "The baby. I named him Jacob."

"It's a fine name," said Jane softly, squeezing his arm.

"It's Nathaniel I worry for," Daniel said sadly. "It worries me how he will cope growing up without a mother."

"You grew up without a mother," Jane reminded him. "And you turned out just fine." She gave him a small smile.

Daniel reached out and covered her hand with his for a moment. Then he pulled away as though suddenly aware of his actions. "Tell me about the shop," he said. "It's doing well, I hear."

Jane smiled. "It is, yes. I owe so much to my generous benefactor." She tried to catch his eye, but Daniel did not look at her. "It brings me great joy to be around flowers all day," she said. "It reminds me of my mother and my childhood."

Daniel smiled, "' *On a bank of flowers, in a summer day.*'"

"Robert Burns," said Jane.

He raised his eyebrows, "You remember it."

"Of course. Many years ago, a wonderful man gave me a wonderful present. We used to read it by the fire together."

Jane could see a smile on Daniel's face. "There was something else," he said. "Something else I gave you with that book. Do you remember? The pressed snowdrop?"

Did she remember? Jane began to laugh gently.

Colour rose in Daniel's cheeks, "I know. It was a silly present."

"A silly present? No, not at all." She stopped walking and looked intently into his eyes. "I'm laughing because you asked if I remember it. I've kept it on my bedside ever since you gave it to me that Christmas."

Jane smiled all the way back to Islington. A great warmth had spread across her chest, making her immune to the bitter cold. How glad she was to have finally seen Daniel again. How glad the silence between them had been broken. And to think he remembered the snowdrop...

In the darkness of the early evening, she brought in the last of the flowers and began to sweep the floor of the shop. She could feel the inexplicable sense of anticipation that hung over the city on Christmas Eve.

It would be twenty years tomorrow, Jane thought distantly. Twenty years since her beloved mother left her in the horror that was the workhouse. She would be glad when tomorrow was over and she did not have to think about Christmas for another year. She hoped that wherever her mother was, she could see the flower shop and she hoped she could see the life Jane had built.

The sound of footsteps yanked her from her thoughts. She looked up to see a young man standing in the doorway. He was well dressed in a blue frock coat and grey scarf, his hair thick and black beneath his top hat. She remembered him coming into her shop in the past, but never at such a late hour.

"I'm sorry," she said, "if you are after flowers, you're a little too late. I'm about to lock up for Christmas."

"You're Jane Walker, aren't you?" the man asked.

"Yes," Jane frowned. Up close, the man had a strange familiarity with him. A previous customer, yes, but there was something more. As he stood close, there was something in his face that drew her to him. Something inexplicable. His cheeks were flushed and unlined, his eyes bright. He looked barely more than a teenager, although he carried himself with the self-assurance of an adult.

The man smiled warmly, "My name is Henry Biesenback, Miss Walker. I've visited your shop on several occasions. You have a fine business here. I particularly like the name. *Roses.*"

Jane smiled crookedly, "Thank you. I named it after my mother."

"I thought it fitting I pay you a visit on Christmas Eve to tell you what a fine job you are doing."

She raised her eyebrows, "A fine job?"

The man's visit was indeed a strange one, but she did not feel threatened. Instead, she felt a strange warmth coming from him and a strange connection between them. There was more to his visit than simply coming to pay her a compliment, of that Jane was sure.

"Who are you?" she asked.

He smiled warmly, "I'm the man who gave you the money for this shop."

CHAPTER 19

Jane stared at Henry in disbelief. "What? You are my benefactor?" She began to pace. She had always believed it to be Daniel. She had always believed the money to have been a way for him to rid himself of her. She let out her breath, thinking of all the energy she had wasted on her anger.

She looked back at Henry. "Why? Why give me money? I'm a stranger to you," she frowned. "Aren't I?"

"Perhaps we might go somewhere to speak?"

Jane nodded, suddenly flustered, "Yes. Yes. Of course. I live above the shop. I can make us some tea." She slid the key into the lock and led Henry through the back of the building to the staircase leading to her apartment. She gestured for him to sit at the small table beside the kitchen. Jane lit the fire and hung the kettle above the flickering flames. He watched her while she worked.

"I noticed you have apprentices," he said.

Jane scooped tea into the pot. "Yes. Two. From the workhouse. Once I was like them," she told him. "A workhouse child. And I am where I am because of the kindness of strangers." She caught his eye. "Not least of all you."

Henry returned her smile.

"It is the least I can do to offer those children the same chance at a future that I have had."

A thin line of steam began to rise from the kettle. Jane poured the boiling water into the pot and filled two cups. She handed one to Henry. He wrapped his hands around the cup and sipped slowly.

After a moment, he said, "I was a workhouse child, too."

Jane's eyebrows shot up. "You? But you're so… You don't look like a…" But as she stumbled over her words, Jane realised why Henry's face seemed so familiar. Why his smile filled her with such warmth. There in front of the fire, she knew she had seen these eyes before. Eyes that had danced with delight as he had presented her with the gift of a doll. He had the face of her father. The smile of her father. The thick black hair of her father.

"I have a present for you. I believe that truly belongs to you." He reached into his coat pocket and pulled out a heart-shaped locket on a gold chain.

Jane shouted out in amazement. The letters J and R were engraved upon it. Intertwined as though they have never been apart. She had not seen it in twenty years.

She stared at it. Speechless for a moment. She opened it with trembling fingers. There inside was her father's hair. She tried to remember everything that had happened twenty years ago. But she was too young. But the reality soon began to hit her.

"You're my brother," she said.

Henry nodded, a faint smile appearing at the corner of his mouth, "Yes."

"You were born in the workhouse. On Christmas morning."

"Yes. Tomorrow is my twentieth birthday."

Jane let out her breath, emotion welling inside her. She put down her teacup, unsure whether she was about to laugh or cry. Perhaps both. She opened her mouth to speak, but nothing came out.

She squeezed her eyes closed, tears threatening behind her eyes.

"Are you all right?" Henry asked gently.

She opened her eyes and smiled. "Yes," she gushed. "Yes, of course. It's just… this is such a shock."

"I'm sure."

"But a happy one," she said, her voice wavering. "A very happy one."

Henry smiled. "I'm glad of it."

"I was sure that you had died that morning along with our mama. The matron did not tell me that you had lived." Jane thought hard, trying to remember the conversation all of those years ago. But she could not.

Jane took a mouthful of tea, the warmth settling her thoughts a little. "Tell me about yourself," she managed.

"I was adopted by a wonderful couple who had emigrated from Germany," Henry told her. "They could not have children of their own and they treated me as their son in every way. I was given a handful of clothes when they took me from the workhouse. I assumed they had been our mother's and, of course that locket. I was told it was my share."

Those words rang a bell in Jane's mind. That is what Mr Weir had said when he brought Emily and the pile of clothing back from the Workhouse after he had officially apprenticed her. It was her share. She should have realised then that there was someone else with whom everything had to be shared. But Matron should have told her this that fateful Christmas day. She should have allowed her to meet her new brother. There was a flash of anger that she had been robbed of the opportunity.

"My adoptive father died a year ago," he continued. "His death prompted me to learn more about my own life, to know more about who I am and where I came from. I knew I had been adopted from the workhouse in Whitechapel so I went back there and requested to see their records. I learned our mother's name was Rose Walker. And I learned she had arrived the day before Christmas Eve. With you.

"They told me you had been taken in by a Mr Weir back when you were a child. I hired Mr Doran, the solicitor, to find you." He clasped his hands around his teacup. "I inherited a fortune when my adoptive father died, Jane. I wanted you to have a share of it. As you said, I was given a chance at a good life through the kindness of strangers; strangers who became my adoptive parents. I wanted you to have a good life, too."

Jane's thoughts were racing. She took another mouthful of tea. "Why didn't you tell me who you were?" she asked. "Why did you not want me to know it was you who had given me the money?"

"I didn't know how you would react," Henry admitted. "I was a stranger."

"They never told me about you," said Jane. "In the workhouse. They never told me you had survived. I always believed you had died with our mother." A single tear slid down her cheek, the emotion of it all finally slipping out. Henry reached across the table and covered her hand with his. The touch felt natural as though they had known each other their whole lives.

"Tell me about her," said Henry. "Our mother."

Jane smiled through her tears. "She was wonderful. She was so loving and warm and would have done anything for anyone. When I was a child, we used to play in the garden together at our house. I named my shop after her because she loved flowers so much."

Henry grinned. "So do you, I see."

"I had always dreamt of owning a flower shop," Jane told him. "And now, thanks to you, it is a reality." She squeezed his fingers. "Thank you." Fresh tears welled inside her. Tears of happiness, she realised.

She had a brother, a family.

No longer was Emily all she had left amongst all she had lost.

"And our father?" asked Henry. "Do you remember him?"

"Of course. He died several months before you were born," she smiled faintly. "He looked a lot like you. It's how I knew who you were." She reached forward and pick up the locket. She paused as she felt the engraving of the initials. Slowly she opened it. That is a lock of his hair. It's the same as yours.

CHAPTER 20

*I*n the morning, Christmas Day, Jane woke to a knock at the door. She sat up sleepily, the sound of the knocker cutting through her dreams. Memories of the previous night came rushing back.

Henry. Her brother.

They had stayed up late into the night, getting to know one another. When he left, Henry had pulled her into his arms and they had clung to each other in a tight embrace as though making up for all the years they had spent apart. The thought of it brought a fresh smile to Jane's face.

The knock came again. She climbed out of bed and pulled a shawl around her shoulders, hurrying downstairs to answer the door.

Her breath caught in her throat. On the doorstep stood Daniel, his hands clasped in front of him and an earnest look on his handsome face. Jane tugged her shawl tighter around her, suddenly embarrassed about opening the door in a state of near undress.

Daniel smiled at the sight of her. "Good morning, Jane. Merry Christmas to you."

"Merry Christmas to you too," she managed, pushing a stray strand of hair behind her ear self-consciously.

"It's early, I know," Daniel told her, the faint colour that Jane was so fond of rising in his cheeks. "But I had to see you."

She raised her eyebrows, "You did?"

"Come to my house for Christmas Dinner after church," Daniel said bluntly. "Please." He hesitated. "That is, unless you have plans. I—"

"No," Jane interrupted. "I have no plans."

Daniel smiled his dimpled smile. "Then please won't you come?" He stepped forward, reaching tentatively for her hand. "As a guest, of course. Not as a servant."

Jane smiled crookedly, "Your uncle won't like that."

"Then my uncle will just have to mind his own

business," Daniel said firmly. "I rather think I am old enough to make my own choices now."

Jane's grin widened.

"What do you say?" His grip on her fingers tightened a little.

"I would be delighted."

Daniel smiled, "Wonderful. I'll have a carriage arrive at eleven."

THE COACH PULLED up outside Daniel's house. He'd accompanied the carriage to ensure that she didn't decide to change her mind. He stepped out into the snow and offered Jane his hand. He led her down the front path and into the house. For twenty years she had been coming to this house, thought Jane, and this was close to the first time she had entered through the front door. It made her walk with her head held high and her shoulders back.

Daniel's uncle was waiting in the parlour, a glass of brandy in his hand. Nathaniel pottered around beside an enormous Christmas tree. It reminded her of that Christmas with her parents so many years ago. The child was dragging a wooden train across the floor. The sight of them made Jane's nerves return. Daniel gave her arm a reassuring squeeze.

"Uncle, you remember Miss Walker?"

The man looked her up and down. The last time he had seen her, she had been wearing a maid's uniform with a food-stained apron. Now she stood tall in a bustled dark green gown, her red hair piled neatly on top of her head. It gave her the confidence to meet his eyes. "A pleasure to see you again, Mr Weir."

He nodded stiffly, "Miss Walker. I hear you are doing well these days."

"Yes," said Jane. "And I owe it all to my brother."

"Brother?" Daniel repeated, his eyebrows shooting up.

Jane smiled, "Yes. I have much to tell you."

"We'll take a walk," he said, his eyes on her, "after Christmas Dinner."

DINNER WAS A LAVISH AFFAIR; the table was piled high with roast meats and rich gravies, and vegetables of every colour. Once the food had been served, Mrs Cron and the new housemaid sat down to eat with them, which made Jane's heart warm. She caught a few disapproving glances from

Daniel's uncle as he watched the kitchen staff eat with the household. How glad she was that Daniel had ceased being influenced by the man.

When the meal had finished, he stood and turned to Jane, "Perhaps we might take that walk now?"

A glance out the window told her a fine snow had started to fall. She buttoned her cloak and tied her bonnet beneath her chin. Her gloved hand pressed to Daniel's arm, they made their way out into the garden.

"So," he began. "A brother?"

At his words, Jane felt a fresh rush of happiness. She told Daniel of the way Henry had appeared at the shop the previous night and confessed to being her benefactor. She caught Daniel's eyes.

"I always thought it was you. But it seems I have more than one person looking out for me in the world."

He covered her hand with his and gave it a gentle squeeze, "I'm glad of it."

She told him of Henry's upbringing and the way he had been taken from the workhouse without her even knowing of his existence. When she finished speaking, Daniel said, "I would very much like to meet him."

"I'm sure he would like to meet you, too. I've told him a lot about you."

"You have?"

"Of course. You're such an enormous part of my life. You've always been there for me."

Daniel lowered his eyes. "I wish that were true. I know I ought to have treated you better. Not let myself be influenced by my uncle and the rest of society."

Jane touched his arm in a gesture of forgiveness. "What choice did you have in the matter? You had your family name to uphold. As much as we might both have wished otherwise, it would never have been fitting for you to marry your father's household apprentice."

He shook his head, "But the thing is, I never cared who you were, or who I was. I never cared about upholding the family name. I let myself be influenced by my father and then my uncle. I let him talk me into things I didn't believe." He stopped walking. Jane noticed they had arrived at the flower garden. The bare earth glittered in the snow.

"I made a mistake," he said, his eyes meeting hers intently. "And I want to rectify it." He swallowed heavily. "I have always loved you, Jane. Ever since the day I met you right here in the garden."

Jane's throat tightened with emotion, "I have always loved you, too."

"My son needs a mother," said Daniel, his hand in hers. "And I need a wife. And the only person I want is the girl I grew up planting flowers with. My best friend."

A single tear slipped down Jane's cheek. Daniel stepped closer and brushed it away. "I know I have not always treated you right," he said. "But I hope you can find it in your heart to forgive me." He squeezed her hand. "Will you be my wife, Jane?"

She leaned close and pressed her lips to his, the way he had done to her so many years ago. "Nothing would make me happier."

EPILOGUE

Jane stood outside the church and tried to breathe deeply. She smoothed the skirts of her white dress, trying to slow her racing heart.

Henry smiled, "You look perfect. Are you ready?"

Jane nodded, "I'm ready." She could hardly believe such a thing was happening. "No, wait." She reached inside her dress and pulled out her locket. She wanted it to be on display not hidden away. She wanted her parents to be a part of this.

She took a final deep breath.

Was she truly about to marry the man she had loved since childhood? She felt a fresh flood of happiness. She took Henry's arm.

The attendants opened the church doors and Jane gasped in surprise. She had expected few guests to turn out to see Daniel's marriage to a lowly girl from the workhouse. But the church was overflowing with guests, a sea of velvets and silks in every colour. As Jane stepped inside, they met her with smiles. Daniel's uncle was present, watching her intently. He gave Jane a nod and even managed a crooked smile. Mrs Cron watched with Nathaniel in her arms, tears of happiness streaming down her cheeks. The sight of her brought a lump to Jane's throat.

And at the altar stood Daniel. Her heart leapt. She could see the nervousness in his eyes, but also intense happiness. He met her eye and grinned broadly.

And all around the church were the most impressive displays of flowers – *roses, in red, white and yellow.* All was perfect.

With her hand tightly on her brother's arm, Jane began to walk down the aisle, towards the man she would always love.

ALSO BY ROSIE DARLING

THE TWELVE THIEVES OF CHRISTMAS

Two desperate orphans, a gang of street thieves and Christmas memories that are best forgotten.

After the death of her parents, Mary Talbot will do anything to protect her younger brother Jack.

Maggie Shaw runs a gang of orphan street thieves, and the Talbots fall into her clutches.

Christmastime means rich pickings for the pickpockets. But Maggie's ruthless nature means that Christmas is often full of fear and loss.

When her best friend, Bobby, is thrown out of the tenement to die alone on the streets, Mary knows that she and Jack must escape the Whitehall slums.

Mary must decide; plan a dangerous way out or risk another Christmas hanging.

CLICK HERE TO DOWNLOAD

Printed in Great Britain
by Amazon